I0654522

Gary McMillan

Mountain Man

The Beginning

Gary McMillan

Books in the Tye Watkins Series

Border Trouble	Second Chance
The Crossing	Yahzie
Yancey	U.S. Marshal
Desperate Trail	El Diablo
Drums Along the Border	Vendetta
Back To the Rockies	A Reason To Kill

Books on Audio

Books in Motion Spokane Valley, Wa.

Border Trouble	Back to the Rockies
The Crossing	Second Chance
Yancey	Yahzie
Desperate Trail	U.S. Marshal
Drums Along the Border	

Mountain Man Series

Published by: Authors Discovery

Published: February 2020

ISBN Number: 978-0-9971107-3-9

Ben Watkins

In

Mountain Man

Book One

By: Gary McMillan

Cover Concept

By

Michael McMillan

Authors Discovery

Gary McMillan

Odessa, Texas

Forward

The following pages are an introduction to a new series that many of my readers have suggested to me. The Tye Watkins Series will continue but in between books will be written about his father, Ben Watkins, trapper or as the early novelist called them, Mountain Men.

The fur industry (mainly beaver) flourished from the early 1800's and started declining around 1835 with the decline of demand for the beaver fur and was over by 1850. During this short time in history the legend of the mountain man was born.

These men were a special breed of men who wanted adventure and the freedom to do what they wanted to do when they wanted to do it. They wanted no one telling them what to do or how to do it. There were no doctors in the Rockies and no law other than trapper law which was pretty simple murder another trapper or steal from another trapper, the penalty was a quick death.

About 3,000 trappers roamed the mountains during those years. Most only lasted two or three years and gave it up or were killed. The historical figures show that about one in five were killed or died of sickness or infection. The only men who got rich were the fur company's owners who bought the furs from the trappers cheap and sold them for high profits. A average trapper who came to the yearly rendezvous where they sold their furs and after purchasing powder, lead, flour, sugar, coffee, traps, and other essentials they would need to survive another year were lucky to have much more than a couple hundred dollars left for a year's work. Some did well but most just made a living. It was a living though, living with a great sense of freedom.

Put yourself in their shoes and ask yourself if you could have done what they did. Some lived and trapped alone while others trapped in parties of five to ten men. These were known as free trappers, men who worked for themselves. The others worked for the fur companies and there was no love lost between the free trappers and the company men.

You would live year around in the mountains facing harsh winters of snow, blizzards, and below zero temperatures for months on end. You would have to survive hostile Indians who resented you coming into their land and killing their game. You would have to face the greatest danger of all, the fearsome grizzly or 'grizz' as the trappers called them. A simple broken leg or other injuries could kill you. There were no doctors in the mountains, so you had to nurse yourself back to health if you were hurt or sick. To survive one had to have keen senses and knowledge of local herbal remedies besides possessing a passel of guts to go along with being able to handle a gun, tomahawk, and knife.

Many men survived years of this dangerous lifestyle and history would show just how important they were to the advancement of western civilization. They discovered passes through the mountains that thousands of men, women, and children would later use to travel to and settle the land west of the Rockies all the way to the Pacific Ocean.

Men like Jim Bridger, Jim Baker, John Coulter who discovered Coulters Hell now known as Yellowstone Park, Kit Carson and many others survived many years in the "Shinning Mountains" known as the Rockies.

This new series will follow Ben Watkins from St Louis to the mountains. It will cover a time in his life from an eighteen-year-old greener (tenderfoot) to the time of his death when his son Tye was twenty-seven years old. During those years he had novels written about him while in the mountains trapping and later became famous along the Texas/Mexico Border when he rode with the Texas Rangers.

I hope you enjoy the series as much as you have enjoyed the Tye Watkins Series.

BEN WATKINS

BOOK ONE

MOUNTAIN MAN

THE BEGINNING

Chapter One

"Wal lookee here Jason. This here young'un must think he's Jim Bridger." The man, Will Hendricks, was making fun of the youngster who was dressed out in new buckskins, new coonskin hat, butcher knife, tomahawk, and carrying a Hawken rifle.

"You know Will," Jason said. "That just about the most fearsome looking man I ever did see," he said laughing and slapping his leg.

The teenager tried to ignore the two and tried to walk by them but the one named Will stuck out his leg and tripped him. The youngster hit the boardwalk hard but was up in an instant.

If you two want trouble you just found it," he said and hit Jason with a right that knocked them man several feet backwards. He handed his rifle to a woman who was standing there. "Hold this for me ma'am. It won't be but a minute. A large crowd of people were watching now and most of them knew the two men to be nothing but troublemakers.

By this time Jason had stepped up and swung a right fist at the young man's head. The teenager blocked the blow with his left forearm and unleashed a vicious upper cut with his right that landed flush under Jason's chin. The crack of knuckle hitting bone could be heard several feet away and Jason was unconscious before his back hit the boardwalk.

Will, recovered from the surprise punch thrown by the young man confronted him again but this time he had his knife out. I'm gonna teach you a lesson you son-of-a-bitch and it's gonna be the last one you will ever get.

The teenager stepped back from a slashing right that held the knife sucking in his belly as he did. He pulled his own 10" butcher knife and dropped to a crouch holding the knife low, cutting edge up like his father had taught him. Will slashed again and the sound of steel hitting steel could be heard as the teenager parried the others blade.

A little frustrated, Will thrust straight at the boy's heart stepping forward as he did so. The youngster stepped back and slashed up from down low and the razor-sharp point of his blade struck Will just below the elbow. Will screamed in pain and dropped his knife grabbing his arm with his left. The teenager ended the fight with a right fist flush on the older man's nose crushing the nose and knocking the man out.

"Somebody get a doctor for these two gentlemen," he said wiping his blade on Will's shirt. A round of laughter followed by backslapping.

"Serves those two right," a man in the crowd said. They have been bullying people for weeks," he added.

Another said, "Well they might better be a little more careful who they bully in the future."

Eighteen-year-old Ben Watkins had arrived in St Louis yesterday and had been astounded at the number of people living there and that everyone seemed to be in a hurry to get somewhere. He rented a room and intended to stay here three or four days to rest up before he started the long trek to the Rockies which he figured to be a two-month journey.

He had left his home a month ago bound and determined to become a trapper like the men he had read about in the dime novels. He had just left the store where he had purchased his new "duds" and replaced his old flintlock rifle with the best rifle in existence, the 54 cal. Hawken. He also bought a brace of pistols, a butcher knife and steel blade tomahawk. He bought new knee-high moccasin boots. He had two hundred and fifty-five dollars left to buy supplies, traps, and other essential he would need on his journey from the money he had saved over the last four years hiring out to neighbors back home.

He was big, six feet two in his stockings and was built the way other men only dreamed of. On top of all this, he was extremely handsome with deep blue eyes and coal black hair that fell to his broad shoulders. He was taught to trap, read sign, shoot, and fight by his father who was a man no one messed with back home. He was on his way back to the hotel when he had been accosted by the two men. Their mistake.

A man dressed in buckskins that were well worn approached young Ben. "Names Jim Thompson and who mite you be?"

Ben took the man's hand noticed it was the hand of a man who was used to using them. "Ben Watkins."

"How old you be boy?"

"Eighteen. Why do you ask?

"You figure on being a trapper," he asked looking at the boy's clothes from top to bottom.

"Yes sir. Fixing to get supplies and a pack horse and head toward the mountains in couple days or so."

"I'd like to talk to you if can spare a moment," Jim said nodding toward an empty table.

After sitting down with each a beer in his hand Jim said. "I like the way you handled yourself a minute ago with those two. Where did you learn to fight like that? I mean you are still a youngster but handled yourself like a man who was much older."

Ben laughed. "My pa is quite a man back home. Hard worker, well respected but no one messes with him. He started to teach me to track and read sign at a very early age and then when I was twelve, he taught me how to fight with fist, wrestle, and how to handle a rifle."

"He taught you good from what I just saw. Listen, Ben, I have a party of six men, and we're headed to the Rockies. Most are greeners," he chuckled when Ben looked at him with a questionable look. He added, "Greener's are men who haven't been there before and have never trapped beaver. "

Ben smiled. "I guess I'm what you called, a greener."

Jim smiled. "Anyway, me and James Wilson are the only ones who have been there, and I'd like you to go with us. After we get there if you want to part ways and go it alone that's okay. It's pretty dangerous between here and yonder. Lots of Indians, mainly the damn Sioux, Kiowa, and

Arapaho before you get there and after you get there you have the Blackfeet and Utes. It would be safer for you to travel with us than going alone and an extra rifle would help us."

After talking a little longer about the mountains Ben was convinced this man knew his way around and could help him with his supplies, knowledge of horseflesh, and maybe tell him something about trapping beaver. There would be lots of time to talk on the journey to the Rockies. He just did not know how much trouble and danger he would encounter before he even got to the foothills of the Rockies and never in his wildest dreams would he ever thought he would become a legend not only in the Rockies but later in Texas.

Chapter Two

The party left St Louis just before daylight the next morning. The leader of the little group, Jim Thompson, felt good about their chances of reaching the Rockies especially with the acquisition at the last minute of the young man, Ben Watkins. He had a feeling about this teenager, a feeling he was going to do great things in the mountains and make a name for himself. He could not explain to himself why he thought this but the feeling in his gut was usually not wrong.

Ben had met and seemed to be accepted by the other members of the party. He was the youngest but the others besides, Thompson and his partner, James Wilson, were not much older. They ranged from twenty to twenty-five. Ben figured Thompson and Wilson were both in their late twenties or early thirties.

It was late May, and the temperature was averaging about fifty degrees during the day and in mid-thirties at night. They traveled primarily at night and camped during the day with only a small fire before daylight for coffee and breakfast. This was Indian Territory. The Arapaho, Comanche, and Kiowa plus some lesser tribes all roamed this country. The primary tribes Kiowa, Comanche, and the Arapaho were the ones they were wary of.

It was perfect traveling weather, and the horses and men were doing well. They were not pushing their mounts and only covering about thirty miles per day. Thompson did not want to follow the Missouri River instead he chose a more direct path due west and would turn north when they reached the foothills of the Rockies. He had been both ways and this trail would save them over two hundred miles. It was a little riskier though with the ever-present fear of being discovered by roving parties of any of the above tribes. A hunting party discovering the shod tracks of the white men's horses would immediately become a white hunting war party.

During the last two weeks Ben had learned a great deal about the men he was traveling with. He had a lot of things in common with Rufus Smith and Billy Clements who were both from Missouri like he was and were farm boys like himself. Rufus was twenty and Billy twenty-one. Neither was big with each being five foot nine, but both were solid built due to all the work required on a farm.

Rufus had red hair that was almost touching his shoulders. He was a good-looking man with blue eyes and light freckles on his cheeks. He was quick to smile, good natured and just a pleasant man to be around and talk to.

He had left the farm much to the displeasure of his ma and pa. He was taught reading and writing and numbers by his ma and had read every dime novel he could find that was about the trappers and the Rockies.

Billy was a black-haired young man who also had blue eyes and was rather common looking. He sprouted a mustache and was pleasant to be around also but was not near as talkative as Rufus was. One could tell he was a fighter just by looking at him; flat nose that had been broken more than once and had a missing tooth in his upper jaw. He had left the farm not by choice but fate; outlaws had visited his home while he was in town on a Saturday night and killed both his parents and after ransacking the cabin, partially burned it to the ground. Billy knew where his pa kept the money box hidden and after burying his parents took the three hundred and fifty dollars that was in the box and headed to St. Louis and the Rockies.

The three young men had formed a friendship and were talking about staying together once they reached the mountains and trapping as partners. They knew, or at least thought they knew the dangers they would be facing and three would be safer than one by himself. They would find out they didn't know doodle-squat about the dangers.

The other two men, Dare Johnson and Jim Taylor were friendly enough but generally kept to themselves. Ben didn't think they necessarily were friends but neither had much to say to anyone else. Thompson and James at times were overly friendly to the youngsters and answered every question during the day when they were holed up hiding from prying eyes.

On the morning of the sixteenth day as they were making camp after another night of riding Ben had a feeling something was wrong. He walked over to where Jim and James had their bedrolls spread out.

"I have a feeling we are in some trouble, Jim," he said.

"What kind of trouble," Jim asked.

"Dunno Sir," he replied, "But I think we had better be looking over our shoulder the way we come."

James spoke up. "We haven't any sign of trouble, not a redskin of any tribe. Go get some rest Ben."

"I think I will stand watch for a while," Ben answered. "With this feeling I couldn't sleep any way."

"Have it your way then," James said and rolled over on his side. Jim sat there for a moment wondering about what Ben said. He watched Ben till as he disappeared over the side of the arroyo, they were in. He sat there for a moment then lay down and was soon asleep thinking *crazy kid*.

Ben was tired and figured he should get some rest while he could, but he just could not shake the feeling that they were in danger. He had been watching for about an hour and was almost falling asleep when movement caught his eye. Instantly alert he watched the back trail, straining his eyes for anything. Sweat stung his eyes and he wiped his face with the sleeve of his buckskin shirt.

Movement caught his eye again. He had not noticed anything before because the Indian was unmoving and blended in with the terrain. As he watched the Indian turned and motioned with his arm as if he wanted someone to join him. A few seconds later he was shocked with several more joined the one he had been watching, As he watched the scout or whatever he was pointed with his bow directly at where they were camped. Ben slid down the side of the ravine and hurried over to Jim and James. He shook Jim's shoulder and the man's eyes flew open.

"Indians Jim. They are on our trail."

"God almighty," he exclaimed rolling out of his bedroll. "How many?

"Not sure but at least a dozen or so."

"Get the others up and ready."

"Yes Sir," he said. He didn't have to as they had heard the commotion and were scrambling getting their weapons together.

In a tone just loud enough for them to hear Jim said. "Don't show yourselves or fire your rifles till I say so. They may not know exactly where we are. He hoped the last statement might calm the youngsters down, but he knew better. Those damn redsticks knew exactly where we were, and he knew we were in for it.

Jim peered over the edge of the ravine and saw his thoughts were confirmed. They had dismounted and were approaching where they were on foot. *Must be some young'uns,* Jim thought as the Indians were bunched up instead of spreading out like seasoned warriors would do.

Jim whispered. "They are fifty yards out. When I say the word fire your long guns and then your pistols. You won't have time to reload so make your shots count." He looked again and yelled "Now." All hell broke loose!

Chapter Three

Seven rifles fired almost as one and three Indians hit the rocky ground never to move again. Two more were hit in the shoulder and were out of the fight. The attackers let loose a volley of arrows at the hated white men. A few seconds later the sound of the men's pistols blasted the air and three more fell to the hard ground and twitched a couple times and were still.

The remaining braves were over the rim of the ravine and it was hand to hand, knives, and tomahawks. Ben was facing a man he noticed was not as old as he at least by his looks, but there was no doubt of his intentions to kill him. Ben blocked a swipe at his belly and slashed up with his knife and the blade cut deep across the brave's throat. Dropping his knife, the Indian grabbed his throat with both hands, blood spurting between his fingers and dropped to his knees for a couple seconds and then fell forward his face hitting the rocks. One leg twitched and then nothing.

Jim saw Ben kill the Indian but then he was busy himself. A brave leaped from the rim of the ravine and hit him like a charging bull buffalo. Jim was knocked backwards against the opposite wall and was stunned. He was looking at sure death as the warrior had his tomahawk raised and was fixing to split his skull when all of a sudden, the man's head exploded, and he collapsed on top of him. Jim glanced to his left and saw Ben holding his still smoking pistol.

Ben had seen the warrior leap at Bill and knock him down and he pulled his second unfired pistol from his belt and fired at the Indian just as the man was going to bash Jim's head. Looking around he saw two of his friends down, dead or wounded he did not know, but he saw Rufus grappling with the lone remaining Redskin. Ben threw his knife at the man's back and saw it bury to the hilt in his lower back. The man turned toward Ben and took one step before Rufus was on him slashing and stabbing.

Ben pulled Rufus off the dead man. "It's over Rufus," he hollered. "It's over. The man is dead." Rufus had a wild, desperate look in his eyes but soon calmed down and started looking around. No more attackers could be seen.

Jim and James walked over to where Ben and Rufus stood. Jim stuck out his hand to Ben which Ben took. Jim held the shake and said, "I had a feeling about you Ben. I had a feeling you were something special and by God you proved it today. Your feeling of danger saved our sorry hides. Without your warning we would have been meat for the buzzards and other varmints.

James stuck out his hand. "Just wanted to thank you my own self Ben." He turned to Jim." We had better check on the rest of the boys. Ben, why don't you and Rufus make sure all those redsticks are dead."

Jim Taylor was dead, an arrow protruded from the middle of his chest. Billy Clements had a knife stuck in his shoulder and would be hurting for a while but would live. Dare was unscathed. None of the Indians were alive in the ravine. Ben and Rufus reloaded their pistols and crawled out to make sure there were none alive out of the ravine. They found the two who were wounded in the shoulder and one attacked Rufus who quickly shot him in the chest. Ben had the other one disarmed and was leading him back to the ravine. Just before he stepped down into the cut the Indian broke and ran. James had reloaded his long rifle and took aim and shot at him. The bullet hit him in the back and the force of the heavy fifty caliber lead ball knocked him several feet forward hitting the ground and rolling over twice and lay still.

Jim said. "We need to find their ponies. If one gets loose and goes back to the village, they will backtrack him and we'll have a whole damn passel of them on us. Let's get the dead Injuns in this ravine and out of the open ground.

Ben spoke up. "If we tie the ponies to a rope and let them follow us it may help cover our shod horses' tracks."

"That might just work," James said looking at Jim. He looked back at Ben. 'Good thinking Ben."

James left to find the ponies. Jim who knew that Ben had killed at least four of the Indians looked at Ben. "Boy, are you sure you are just eighteen?" He slapped Ben on the back.

Thirty minutes later, the dead Indians where partially hidden in the ravine and Taylor was buried in a shallow grave with rocks piled on top to keep the varmints away. Camp was broke and for the first time they traveled during the day. Ben and Rufus had the ropes leading the Indian ponies.

Rufus spoke up. "Do you know what tribe those Indians were from?"

"Not really," Ben answered. "I think they were Kiowa, maybe Arapaho. I don't think they were Comanche."

Rufus nodded his head. "I'll ask Jim when we make camp.

Many miles behind them and a little north of their back trail Little Wolf sat on his pony with his friend Spotted Tail.

"I think maybe the young ones are in trouble Spotted Tail. They should have been back here by now."

"I have been thinking the same thing my brother. Maybe we should follow their trail and find out." The two friends along with several of the others kicked their ponies into a trot and left their camp following the young one's tracks.

Several hours later and about twenty-five miles or so from where the fight took place the group of trappers made camp. It was a good camp and even the younger men could see why Jim and James had picked this spot. It had a small spring coming out of the base of the sixty-foot sheer rock wall behind them with an overhang at the top preventing anyone shooting down on them from the rim. Plenty of large boulders lay around where they would be offering plenty of protection from the front or sides. The area in front and to the left and right was clear of any brush or rocks big enough for a man to hide behind. Another good thing was that they were on high ground and anyone attacking them would be fighting an uphill battle. The loose shale that covered the area would not only slow the horses down but would help the guard on night duty hear anyone trying to sneak upon the camp.

The small fire was hid among the rocks and dead wood used to help keep down the smoke from being seen even though it would too dark to see it in about thirty minutes. Coffee was made and poured into the damnable tin cups. It was good coffee-black, hot, strong, and thick enough to almost allow a spoon to stand up in it.

"Jim," Rufus said, "Ben and me was wondering what tribe those Indians were today."

"Boys, you just had your first encounter with the Kiowa, and I will be willing to bet it won't be your last before we get to those mountains."

"I noticed how young those men were," Ben said. "I figure you think the older ones will find them and follow us."

"Sure as God made little green apples," James said. "That's the main reason we took our time finding this here place to camp. Figured it to be a good place to hole up and wait for them. Got plenty of cover, water handy, and lots of lead and powder. If they come at us here, they might get us after a while but it's going to be mighty costly for them."

"You boys might as well get used to finding camps that is defendable." Jim said. "When you are in those mountains you can't let your guard down for a second. Keep your fires small and hidden by rocks or in a hole. A fire can be seen a long ways. Always, and I mean always reload you rifle or pistol as soon as possible after firing it. The best weapon ain't worth a tinkers damn if you need it and it ain't loaded. Keep your eyes moving at all times. Remember, if you see sunlight reflecting off something it's probably man made. "

James added. "If you get yourself in a fight remember one thing. The one who moves first is the one usually killed. Learn patience and be still. It's easy to see something moving but not so easy something that is not. Use your eyes and ears boys and if you have to turn your head or move a leg or something to get a little more comfortable do it slow, real slow. Another thing, if you see your enemy do not stare at him, look at him out of the corner of your eye."

Why is that" Rufus asked?

Ben spoke up. "My pa told me that a real fighting man can sense when someone is watching him."

Rufus chuckled. "That's crazy man."

Jim looked at Rufus. "Ben's pa was right Rufus. A real fighting man can sense that. I've actually had that experience before and still have my hair because of it."

"Well I never would have thought that. I thought if you saw your enemy you never took your eyes off him."

Jim chuckled. "You don't son, you just don't stare directly at him."

James stood up and walked over to where his saddle bags were and took out his possible bag. He fumbled around in it till he found what he was looking for. He came back a sat down and took his butcher knife from the sheath on his belt and started stroking it on the flat rock he had gotten from his possible bag.

Note: The possible bag was carried by the mountain men since generally their pants had no pockets. They carried their flint and steel, pipe and tobacco, skinning knife, extra powder and lead balls and patches, extra flint for his weapons and anything else he thinks he might need.

In a few minutes James was satisfied he had a good edge when he shaved some hair off his arm. It was full dark now and the fire had been put out but not before everyone had one last cup of coffee.

"How much farther to the mountains Jim," Billy asked through clinched teeth. He was hurting something fierce from the knife wound in the shoulder. Outside of a little whiskey there was nothing the others could give him for the pain.

"Probably about two maybe three weeks if we don't run into too much more trouble with the Indians or rain that swells the creeks and rivers so we can't cross them," Jim replied.

Ben said. "Jim, you and James been giving us lessons on how-to survive in the mountains just about every camp. How about telling us about the mountains, what they look like, animals that live there."

James laughed and answered. "I can answer that for you Ben. There ain't nothing on God's green earth that can compare to the majesty of the Rockies. Some days you can't see the tops because of the clouds. Most have snow on the tops year around. The tall pines the beautiful aspens make fine decor for your camps. Green meadows with grass waist high, cold clear creeks everywhere from the melting snow in summer and beaver in all of them." He took a couple of puffs on the pipe he had filled, lit it and said. "You youngun's remember this-along about October or before the big cold sets in find you a place to hole up for two or three months. It's going to be ass deep snow or deeper and cold-cold like you ain't ever seen before for weeks and weeks. Pile up plenty of firewood and stock up on meat because game gets scarce in the wintertime. Kill you one or two of the mountain buffalo before the cold sets in and make you a coat and a blanket."

Jim cut in the conversation. As far as game goes you have the mountain buffalo, deer, elk, turkey, black bear, big horn sheep, coyotes, mountain lion, moose, the wolves, and of course the Lord of the Mountains, the damnable Ole Ephraim better known as the grizzly bear along with a hundred other smaller varmints including what you are looking for, beaver."

"Why with all the other animals you mentioned why do you refer to the Grizzly as damnable," Rufus asked.

"Because Son," Jim answered, "Ole Ephraim has probably killed as many trappers as the Blackfoot and the Ute. A big one can stand ten-foot-tall on its hind legs and is as temperamental as a woman. You come up on her and she might charge you immediately or she may just sniff the air and figure you smell too bad to eat." Both he and James laughed heartily at that remark. "Truth is boys, just stay the hell away from them if you can. If you can't do that don't try and run because he will catch you quickly. The best thing to do is stand your ground make yourself as big as you can by raising your arms over your head and start yelling your lungs out. Sometimes that will make him uneasy enough to go away."

"And if he don't," Rufus stated.

"Then boy," Jim said in a solemn voice, "Prepare to meet your maker." Rufus swallowed hard.

"Getting on to nine o'clock boys we had better turn in," Jim said. "Rufus you take the first watch and Ben you relieve him at midnight. Dare will relieve you and then James and I'll take the last watch. Stay awake and don't doze off. Billy you just rest up."

"Why are both of you taking the last watch," Ben asked.

"Injuns are notional people." Jim said. "Most times they won' fight at night but one just can't tell. Normally, if they are going to attack an enemy, they will hit at first light. I figure two sets of eyes at that time are better than one.

"I can stand watch," Billy said. "Damn shoulder hurts too much to sleep."

Bill tossed him a half full bottle of rot gut. Drink it up and you won't feel much and get some sleep. We are going to need you gun before long." Billy caught the bottle, nodded his head and took a hefty swallow, then another and before long was out light like a light.

Not far from the trapper's camp Little Wolf, Spotted Tail and fifteen other very angry Kiowa warriors were eating pemmican waiting for the moon to come up so they could see the tracks of the men they were chasing. The idea of using the Indian ponies to cover their tracks was a good one but was also working in the favor of Little Wolf. That many ponies were easy to follow much more so than the five ponies of the trappers would have been. What they did not know was the white men had cut the ponies loose.

They had found where the fight took place earlier in the day. It did not take long by reading sign that they knew exactly what happened. Most of the warriors with him now were battle tested but four or five were young and inexperienced. Little Wolf explained to them the mistakes the young ones had made so they would remember and not make them again.

The band was on the trail again and moving at a fast pace since so many horses was like following one of the white man's trails the wagons traveled on. When the sun was coming up and the darkness fading across the land they stopped to study things a little closer. Almost at once Spotted Tail, the best tracker in the band, knew something was wrong. He looked up at Lone Wolf who still sat on his pony.

"We are close to the horses, but I do not think the white men are still with them. In our haste we overlooked them leaving the ponies of our brothers."

"How could we miss five or six horses leaving?" Lone Wolf questioned.

"I think these are experienced fighting men. They left the trail one at a time so we would not notice." Spotted Tail jumped on his pony.

"We will go back and find where the last one left the trail and follow him," Lone Wolf said. He led the party back down the trail.

"You are going to make a hell of a trapper Ben," Jim Thompson said while sipping coffee. First of all, you have that knack for smelling out trouble and then you think of ways to get out of trouble. Leading those Indian ponies to cover our tracks was good thinking and then having us leaving one at a time was even smarter."

"Thanks Jim, but to tell you the truth I think it only slowed them down. From what I have heard and from what my pa told me the Indian are trackers second to none. They will figure out what we did and be back on our trail. I think the idea only slowed them but will not fool them for long."

"So, when do you expect them to show up?"

"About first light. They will find where we rendezvoused and then five shod ponies won't be hard to follow especially since we had almost a full moon. I expect we had better fort up, get a little rest and be ready."

"Why don't we move out and keep going, try and stay ahead of them," Dare asked.

Jim answered. "Wouldn't be a bad idea if our mounts weren't so worn out. You get on foot our here and it's a sure death warrant."

No one said anything for a moment as they squatted around the fire sipping coffee and then Jim spoke up.

"I think Ben here is right. We only slowed those devils down and they are on our trail right now and smelling blood, our blood for those we killed back on the trail."

"What the hell do you think we should do then," Dare asked.

All of the men stared at their leader waiting for a answer. "Fort up," he said. Starting right now find you a place and dig yourself a hold and pile some rocks around it and not just in front but especially behind you to protect your back. Have your long rifle, pistol, knife and tomahawk handy. If you are a believing man, I suggest you talk to the Man upstairs and make peace with Him. We all knew the possibility of something like this happening so good luck and watch each other's back." The men scrambled to find a place to do as Jim said. Ben dug out a hole large enough for himself and his wounded friend Billy. Between the two they had two long rifles and four pistols. They settled in and all knew it was going to be a long sleepless night.

Chapter Four

Little Wolf and Spotted Tail had found where the white men had met up and were on their trail with fifteen seasoned warriors that only had one thing in mind, white man's blood.

"We should rest our ponies Little Wolf," Spotted Tail said. "From the tracks we should catch up with them tomorrow, but our ponies need to be fresh."

Little Wolf looked at his friend and knew he was right. He knew he should have thought of that, but hate had clouded his thinking. He held up his hand and reined in his mount.

"We will rest our ponies and we will eat," he told all. "We will catch the white men tomorrow." The ponies were picketed, and the braves dug out some pemmican from the deerskin pouch each carried. The pemmican was made from pounded up meat and mixed with fat to make a cake type food that was both nutritious and filling. Certain herbs could be added for flavor.

Little Wolf and Spotted Tail sat a small distance from the others so they could talk. They had been friends for as long as each could remember and had spent many nights away from their camp. Mostly as those times they talked of the things their fathers had said about the old days when they had been out with their fathers.

Stories about the buffalo hunts where the number of buffalo were more than one could count. Stories of if one was hidden and watching the buffalo move by where they were hidden it would take half a day for the first one to the last one to pass. Their fathers told them stories of battles with the Sioux, Cheyenne, and Pawnee which were the Kiowa's mortal enemies since before they could remember. The Kiowa, Plains Apache, and the Comanche had formed a coalition and sometimes banded together to fight these tribes.

These were the old days when raiding their enemy's camps and stealing their horses and sometimes their women were common happenings. They still occurred occasionally as both Little Wolf and Spotted Tail had won great respect in their tribe for their bravery but most of the fighting now for all the tribes of the plains Indians were against the invading wave of white eyes that were beginning to force their way into their lands.

Little Wolf shouted suddenly at Stalking Coyote to come to where he and Spotted Wolf sat. Spotted Wolf wondered why his friend had done this and Little Wolf spoke to him while he wondered what was going on.

"The thought came to me that we should send a warrior to find the white man's camp so we can plan for the best way to kill them."

Stalking Coyote came to them and sat down. Little Wolf spoke to him.

You are the best tracker among us. I would like you to go on ahead and find the white man's camp and come back and tell us what you found so we do not make the same mistake the others made. I do not think they are very far ahead of us." Stalking Coyote stood up, nodded his head and walked to his pony without saying a word.

Ben figured it was a little after midnight. He looked at Billy and could tell his friend was in some pain. He nudged him slightly.

"Lay back and try to get some sleep. I'll keep watch."

"Don't know if I can Ben. Damn shoulder is still hurting something fierce."

Ben lifted the bandage and took a look at the knife wound. It didn't look good as it was turning red around the cut indicating infection.

"Jim" he said just loud enough for the man to hear. "We have any of that rot gut left that I can pour on Billy's wound?"

"Maybe a half bottle. He reached in his saddle bag that he had taken to his hole and took the bottle out.

"Here," he said and tossed the bottle the five or six feet to where Ben was.

Ben caught the bottle and pulled the cork and lifting the bandage he poured some of the liquid on the wound. Billy didn't shout out in pain but he sure as hell felt the burning in his shoulder. Ben poured a little more and Billy, his cheeks puffed out and teeth grinding fell back passed out. *Best thing that could happen to him*, Ben thought to himself.

Unknown to the party of white men a pair of black eyes watched them from only fifty feet away. Stalking Coyote surveyed the camp making mental notes of each man's location. He immediately knew these were warriors by their defensive positions they set up. It would make it dangerous for an open attack. He backed away for fifty or so yards and then walked the quarter mile to his pony.

An hour later he arrived back to the camp. Little Wolf came up to him before he slid off his pony. "Did you find their camp?'

Stalking Coyote nodded and squatted on the ground. Picking up a stick he scratched out the camp of the white men. He held up five fingers on one hand and one finger on the other indicating how many men were in the camp. "One man is injured, and I don't think he can help fight."

Little Wolf studied the layout of the camp drawn in the dirt and drew the same conclusion Stalking Coyote had. The men had scratched out holes in the dirt and rocks and were facing in all directions, not just one so whatever direction the warriors attacked they would meet the white men's rifles.

He had the other warriors gather around. "We are but a short distance behind the white men's camp. Where they are, we would lose many warriors if we attacked them. So, this is what we will do. Stalking Coyote will go back and watch the camp. We will go with him and stop when we are very close and wait for him to return with what they are doing. When we know what direction, they are going we will get ahead of them and set up a trap that they cannot escape." This was followed by much shouting and excitement. Little Wolf held up both of his hands and the men quieted down. "Tomorrow we will avenge out brothers. Let us go."

"Where are they," Dare asked to no one in particular. The sun was over the eastern hills and no sign of any Red Sticks as Dare called the Kiowa.

"I've got to piss something fierce Rufus said," and stood up from his hole and picking up his rifle walked away from camp a few yards. Standing there relieving his bladder he looked around and almost shouted out a warning but managed to stifle his scream. He got a glimpse of an Indian just as the man ducked behind some rocks. He managed not to stare at the place he had seen him and finished his business. Picking up his rifle he had leaned against a large boulder he turned and walked as calmly as he could back to camp. It was the longest thirty seconds of his life. As he walked, he expected an arrow in the back at any second.

Reaching his friends, he softly told them. "Don't look around. I think I spotted a Red Stick while I was peeing. He ducked out of sight and I did not see him again, but I don't think I was seeing things.

Jim asked. "If it was did, he know you seen him?"

"I'm not sure," Rufus answered. "I tried not to let him know."

"Get back in your hole. We'll have to wait and see."

Stalking Coyote was furious at himself for falling asleep. There had been nothing he could do about what happened. He woke up to the sound of a stone being kicked and saw the white man relieving himself not fifty steps from where he lay. He was not sure if the man saw him or not, so he lay there and did not move. He heard the man walking away and glanced over the rocks and bushes. The man was talking to the others, but no one seemed alarmed. As he watched the man walked over to his hole and lay down.

An hour later it was apparent to the men there would be no attack. "We can't stay here all day," Jim said. "Let's pack up and get the hell out of here." Five minutes later the little party was moving out toward the west and the Rockies. Ben rode last in line and was watching their back trail for any sign of trouble coming their way. To a man they believed Rufus had seen a Kiowa warrior and

Gary McMillan

each knew they were not out of trouble. Out here in this country you were never far from it. Trouble was always lurking around or over the next hill.

Chapter Five

Jim called a halt to rest the horses at mid-morning. As far as rest goes the men probably needed it more than the horses since the horses slept and rested all night while the men with the exception of Billy slept none at all.

"Seen any dust or any signs we are being followed Ben," he asked.

Ben shook his head. "No, I haven't, but I got me a feeling we are."

"The hair on the back of my neck is standing up," James said. "That usually means trouble is close by."

"Hell man!" Dare blurted out. "I'm tired of this crap of the hair on the back of my neck, gut feelings and all this other bullshit coming from ya'll. Believe what you see and nothing else is what I believe." He walked a few feet from where the others were and begin unbuttoning his pants to relieve himself. Two arrows hit him in the chest and protruding six inches out his back. He turned and started to say something, and another hit him in the back. He was dead when he hit the rocky ground.

"Get mounted!" Jim shouted leaping in his saddle.

Ben helped Billy on to his saddle and was getting mounted on his own horse when an arrow whizzed by him and hit Billy in the throat. Billy grabbed his throat with both hands as blood spurted out his mouth and between his fingers. He fell backwards off his horse. Knowing nothing could be done for his friend Ben lay low in the saddle and kicked his horse into an all-out run chasing Bill and the others praying no arrows struck his mount or his pack horse. Luck was with him as all escaped the trap except Dare and Billy. Their mounts and pack horses had followed the other horses with saddle bags, possible bags, and stirrups on the two horses of Dare and Billy's flapping wildly. Somehow when after about a mile run, they all slowed to a walk everything was still on the horses. An arrow was stuck in one of the saddle bags on one of the pack horses but did not go all the way thru as it hit a bag of lead balls.

"We'll walk them for a while and let them catch their wind. If the damn Kiowa show up, they will at least have some bottom left if we have to make a run for it." Jim looked around at the men. "Where's Billy?"

"I was helping him on his horse and an arrow caught him square in the throat."

"Damn those heathens to hell," Jim cursed. "Keep a sharp eye out." They continued on their way with all looking in every direction.

Ben looked at his friends. Seven counting his own self started out and now there were four. Anyone else might have doubts creeping into his mind about whether it was worth it considering what had happened so far but not Ben. This was something he had dreamed of for the last three years and Indian trouble was part of being a trapper and he accepted it. If he was destined by the Man upstairs not to make it to the mountains-then so be it.

Jim held his mount back and let Ben catch up to him.

"These Kiowa know this land like the back of their hand," he said. "They decided what direction we were going and got ahead of us and set that ambush. Got me a feeling they are getting ahead of us again."

"Been thinking the same," Ben answered. "Is there another trail we can take and maybe fool them temporally? It would at least buy us some time before they figured things out."

"Let me think on it." They rode on.

Little wolf and his band of warriors had taken short cuts that they knew well and were already well ahead of the party of white men. They had set their trap on a well-known trail they figured the white trappers were going to follow. Little Wolf expected their quarry to be here just before dusk. He had four warriors with him and was blocking the trail. Spotted Tail had four men with him to the north and the others were on the south side of the trail. Instructions were given to stay hidden and not show themselves until the signal came from Little Wolf. They waited patiently for the white men so their quest for revenge would end. Each hoped one or two of the men would still be alive so they could find out just how brave the white men were... or how cowardly they were.

"I've been studying this map," Jim tapped the side of his head with his finger indicating where the map was, "And there ain't no good way to go except the trail we're on. To swing more north is going to put us trying to figure out how to cross some wide, deep rivers, at least two."

"I don't figure we can make it with the pack horses and camp gear we have. Plus, that's Sioux country and they are a hell of a lot more dangerous than the Kiowa. There's a lot more of them than most tribes and a war party is going to be twice or more size than the one we are facing with the Kiowa now."

"So, you're thinking we take our chance with the Kiowa," Ben replied.

"I don't think there is more than twelve or fifteen of them. We are outnumbered three or so to one, but we have the firepower and they have bows."

Ben said. "They are pretty damn accurate with them from what I've seen so far. I can understand your thinking if things were different and we were fighting from a distance, but this is going to be close in fighting and they are deadly with those bows and arrows in that situation. You seen what happened to Dare when he was going to pee."

"Hell, I know that Ben. I saw Dare take those three arrows faster than a man can spit but that don't change the fact we are in a pickle. It's dammed if we go where we are headed and dammed if we swing north. I just don't know."

"Well, let's just keep going, keep our eyes peeled for an ambush spot and then just kick our mounts and run like hell through it and hope for the best."

"I figured as much from you. Don't know anything except tackle a problem head on," Jim chuckled. "Let's get the men together and tell them the situation."

The men didn't have much to say. They understood the situation and let Jim make the decision on what they would do. They mounted up and continued west each man watching for signs of trouble.

Eyes stung from the sweat rolling down their faces and shirts stuck to their backs like a second skin. Still they moved west. The only sound was the creaking of saddles and the hooves striking the ground and an occasional rock. About an hour before sunset they saw it and each man knew that if the Kiowa were still wanting to kill them this was where it was going to happen. Ahead of them a quarter of a mile was gigantic boulders that had been thrown from the bowels of the earth hundreds, maybe thousands of years ago.

Jim gathered the men around him. We can go around the boulders yonder but in the midst of them is a spring and we need water. It's maybe sixty or maybe a little more miles to the next water. We might make it, but horses won't. We are going to hit that pile of boulders in an all-out run. Leave your long rifles in their sheaths and have a pistol in your hand. Hold on to the rope leading your pack horses till after we start running then turn them loose. They will follow the other horses. Lay low and shoot at anything that moves on the ground. Don't stop for anything till you reach the spring then dismount and find a hole to fight them off." He looked at each man. "Good luck.

Thirty yards from the notch in the boulders where the trail entered Jim let out a yell and kicked his horse's flanks. Everyone else slapped or kicked their horses and with all yelling like the devil was after them followed him into hell

Chapter Six

This move of the men charging the boulders surprised Little Wolf and he screamed his war cry. Immediately the others rose from their positions and let loose their arrows. Wilson tumbled off the back of his horse with two arrows in him, one in the chest and one in the side just below his rib cage. He hit the ground hard, raised himself up and shot one of the braves who had shot him then fell face down in the dirt and died.

Ben was close behind Jim and Rufus was hot on Ben's horse's tail. Arrows were whizzing by thick as flies on stink, but the men were moving fast and so far the arrows had missed all but Wilson then Ben heard a yell behind him and turned slightly to glance back. An arrow protruded from Rufus's left shoulder. His pack horse was stumbling with two arrows in him. Rufus was now lying almost flat on his horses back and somehow was staying in the saddle.

Jim's horse stumbled but stayed up with an arrow in his hip. An arrow struck Ben's pommel on his saddle glancing upwards and cut a gash in his right forearm which hurt like hell.

Ben saw the spring ahead but also saw four warriors kneeling in the trail attempting to prevent them from reaching the water. Jim leveled his pistol and fired and was surprised to see one of the warriors fall backwards. To hit anything from a running horse took skill and a lot of luck.

The other three warriors let loose their arrows at less than twenty yards and two hit Bills horse in the chest and he went down throwing Jim to the ground where he hit hard and rolled several times. Ben, being right behind, was holding on best he could as his horse jumped the horse Jim was riding. When his horse had all four hooves on the ground Ben was on top of the warriors. He shot one in the face and his horse knocked one head over heels into the rocks. He heard a pistol bark behind him and knew Rufus had fired at the remaining warrior. Ben was at the spring, leaped off his horse after grabbing his Hawken long rifle and canteen.

Right behind him was Rufus also grabbing his long rifle and canteen. He stumbled some but managed to scramble into the rocks by the spring and collapsed.

Ben, looking back down the trail saw a warrior rushing toward where Jim lay. Sighting his Hawken quickly he squeezed the trigger. The fifty-caliber ball struck the brave in the chest and knocked him five feet thru the air backwards. He was dead before he hit the ground.

Rufus, his left arm useless as far as holding the barrel of his rifle, laid the barrel of his Kentucky long rifle on the boulder in front of him and was searching for a target. Ben reloaded his Hawken and was also watching for any movement. Both had reloaded their pistols. They waited.

Jim lay about twenty yards back down the trail. As Ben looked, he saw him move slightly. Ben shouted.

"Jim, if you can hear me don't move. If the Kiowa think you are still alive, they will fill you full of arrows. If you can hear me barely move your head." He stared at Bills head and saw it move slightly. "Hang on. It will be dark soon and I will try and get you. Just don't move." Ben settled down in the rocks to wait-and watch.

Jim lay there not moving but hurting like hell. He didn't know if his left leg was broken or not, but it felt like it might have been. His left shoulder he was sure was dislocated or broken and his mouth was so dry he could not spit if he wanted to. Apparently, he had been out for a few minutes but did not want to move to feel the left side of his head which also ached like the devil.

Ben while watching for movement was reflecting back some. *Maybe my parents had been right in saying it was a mistake for me to leave the farm and head to the mountains and to God knows what danger. Maybe they had been right,* then he shook his head. *No, this is what I have wanted for a long time regardless of what happens. I want to know the feeling that Bill said all trappers have-*

the feeling of freedom: The feeling of doing things when you wanted to and no man telling you what you need to do. The seeing of things that no white man had seen before. To take in the beautiful mountains, the tall pines and the wildlife that was so plentiful. This is what I wanted more than anything and by God he was going to do it. He made up his mind right there that nothing was going to stop him.

It was full dark now and not a sign of the Kiowa. He worked his way over to a hurting Rufus to look at his shoulder. The arrow was far enough below the collar bone that he figured it missed bone which was a good thing and he told Rufus as much. The flint point protruded about four inches out his back. Ben took his butcher knife and carefully cut the tip off. Without saying anything to Rufus he jerked the shaft back out of the shoulder. Rufus's face turned red and his cheeks puffed out, but he didn't scream.

Ben's horse and pack horse was in the rocks along with Rufus's mount. Ben crawled to where they were and standing up when he got to Rufus's. He reached in the saddle bag and found what he was looking for, a flask of whiskey and a shirt. He got back down on the ground and crawled back to Rufus.

"This is going to hurt like hell fire Rufus, but it's got to be done or the wound will get infected." He picked up a stick about a half inch round and four inches long. "Bite down on this." Rufus put the stick between his teeth and

Ben poured the whiskey in the hold in front hole and then in the back. Rufus passed out. Ben wrapped the wound from strips he cut from the shirt as best he could.

He picked up Rufus's pistol and stuck it in his belt. With his two that gave him three shots which he felt would be sufficient. He started moving toward Jim ever so slowly his eyes searching the boulders for any sign of trouble. When he was close to him, he spoke in just above a whisper.

"Jim, can you hear me?"

"Yeah."

"Can you move your legs?"

"Left one is busted I think." He shifted his body and moved his right leg and then the left which pained him a hell of a lot. He was stiff from lying still for so long, but he could feel the blood beginning to flow in his legs. "Give me a minute and I'll try to get my legs under me and stand up."

Ben was thankful for no moon as it was very dark among the boulders. Of course, it could work against them too as they could not see the Kiowa no more than the Kiowa could see them.

Jim stood up slowly and painfully and put his right arm on Ben's shoulder for support. They moved slowly and silently back to where Rufus was. Reaching him he helped Jim lay down and he squatted between him and Rufus. He picked up his canteen and after letting Jim have a good drink, he poured a little water of Rufus's face waking him up. Ben quickly put his hand over his friend's mouth to muffle any sound. When he felt that Rufus had gotten over the shock of being awaken like that, he removed his hand.

"Listen to me Rufus," Ben whispered. "I know you are hurting but you have got to stay awake and help us fight off these Kiowa are we are all dead. Do you understand?"

Rufus, grimacing, raised himself to a sitting position. Ben helped him slide his butt over some where he could rest his back against a boulder.

"You okay?" Ben questioned

Rufus nodded his head. "You can count on me helping as much as I can. As far as me being okay-hell no!"

Ben took his friends rifle and laid it across the top of a fairly flat-topped boulder in front of Rufus. It would do to brace the rifle since Rufus's left arm was useless. He could reload but not very quickly, so Ben gave him his pistol back plus one of his own.

"You're looking straight down the path we came on. If you see anything move shoot and ask questions later." Rufus nodded his head and shifted some so he could handle the rifle with one hand.

He looked at Jim. "Can you move over there, he pointed to an opening between some boulders that would allow him to cover the left side of the trail?

Ben moved to the other side of the trail and found a place that he could defend the trail to the west and also the right side. His back was protected pretty well. They settled in for a long night.

Little Wolf had been the warrior Ben's horse crashed into. The other three that were with him were all dead, shot by the white men as they rode by. He was in no shape to fight as his right shoulder was badly bruised and his right and leg knee was hurting him something fierce, but true to his warrior heritage he showed no pain. Spotted Tail squatted beside him.

Little Wolf said. "These white men are great warriors especially the big one. We have killed four of them but counting our brothers back on the trail and those here they have killed here is more than three times that number."

"What are you thinking my brother?"

Little Wolf did not answer for a moment. "I think it is enough. We will go back to our camp and our women and children before any more women have to cry for lost husbands or sons."

"Spotted Tail was quiet for almost a minute before he spoke. "I think it is good we go back."

Little Wolf was glad his friend agreed with him. "We will start back when the sun is just coming over the hills.

It was a long night for the three white men. They knew most Indians don't like fighting after dark but these they knew were pretty upset and might just try their luck. Rufus had no problem staying awake because he was in a lot of misery with his shoulder. Jim was pretty much in the same boat with his knee and busted shoulder. Ben stayed awake because he was not only watching where he was supposed to but not knowing if the others could stay alert with the problems they had. He was looking in all directions the whole night. There was no moon but with no clouds the stars helped some. He listened as much as he watched. His ears tuned to the normal night sounds and would instantly be alert if any sound was heard that was not normal. Only once had he been jerked alert by the sound of small pebbles slipping down from above. After straining his eyes and hears for a few minutes he was satisfied it was just normal shifting of the rocks which he knew wasn't a strange occurrence.

When the dark skies begin to turn gray three bleary-eyed, dog-tired men were waiting the attack they knew was coming. Each did not know if they would live to see another sunset, see their home again, live to love a woman, or live to reach their dream-the Rockies.

Suddenly a Kiowa warrior stepped out of the boulders into the trail.

"Don't shoot yet," Jim shouted. "I think he wants something."

"Yeah," Rufus shouted back. "Our scalps."

Jim said again. "Don't shoot."

The warrior, obviously hurt, raised his right hand in the universal peace sign and then started going through sign language using both hands. Bill, the best he could, answered in sign language followed by the peace sign. The warrior turned and left with several more coming out of the rocks joining him as they walked away. A few minutes later they heard the hoof beats of the ponies as they rode away.

"Well, if I live to be a hundred, I'll never figure out Injuns," Jim said laughing.

"What the hell is going on," Rufus asked anxiously? Ben came over to listen.

Jim said. "That warrior was named Little Wolf and he said they had lost warriors and we had lost warriors. Enough of killing. He was leaving."

"He said all of that with those crazy hand signs?" Ben asked.

"Those hand signs are pretty much the same for all the tribes," Jim replied. "You will do well to learn as much as you can about using it. Might just save your sorry hide someday."

Jim said. "I don't know about you two, but I am dead tired. Let's round up what equipment and supplies that's scattered along our back trail that the Kiowa didn't take. We need to take care of my friend James Wilson's body too. After that let's rest up for a while then head out.

Gary McMillan

Chapter Seven

After gathering up what supplies they could find they buried James with Jim saying a few words over his friend. The Kiowa had taken the guns, powder and lead from the pack horse and from James's body sometime during the night. James's horse had come back and had stopped with the others. James's long rifle, powder, lead, coffee and other food stuff would come in handy. The three men let the horses have all the water from the spring they wanted and let them roll in the grass that grew around it. The men stretched out for a little rest themselves. Ben took the first watch, Rufus the second, and Jim the last. Mid-afternoon found them on their way.

The next few days were uneventful, and Rufus and Jim were pretty much over their wounds and injuries. Jim was lucky in that nothing had been broken or dislocated and was mending well. Ben's minor cut on his arm from the arrow that bounced off the pommel of his saddle was totally well thanks to the rot gut that he kept pouring on it. He reminded himself to always have a supply with him, for medicinal purposes only of course. That thought brought a smile to his lips.

Night camps were spent listening to Jim talk of the Rockies. He spoke of the many dangers they would face. He spoke of how important it was to learn the medicinal benefits of many of the plants. Most of all he emphasized how bad the winters could be and the importance of finding a shelter one could hole up in for a few months before the snow began to fall. He assured both Rufus and Ben that they had never seen cold and snow like they were going to experience. He explained more than once how to skin a buffalo, cure the hide and make a coat and a blanket.

"I guarantee you will freeze to death if you do not kill and skin a couple buffalo so make finding them a priority early on. Make sure you have plenty coffee and meat for the winter. It will be cold enough you don't have to worry about it spoiling. Game becomes hard to come by in dead of winter as is firewood so stock up. Ben also was practicing his sign language skills that Bill was teaching him almost every night and he was feeling pretty comfortable with it.

On about the thirty-fifth day, Ben wasn't sure exactly how many, since they left St. Louis they come across a herd of buffalo. This was the first that Ben and Rufus had ever seen and was shocked at how big they were. Jim explained that these plains buffalo were a lot bigger than the mountain buffalo, so they were going to try and kill three or four of them. That would give them a hell of a lot of meat and hides to make coats from.

"Are all the herds this big," Rufus asked looking at the herd which probably had five or so hundred buffalo?

Jim laughed. "This here herd is very small compared to some I have seen. Your big herds would stretch as far as the eye could see and could take a half day to move past where you were." He didn't say anything else for a few seconds "These buffalo could be a gift from above," he commented.

They were downwind when Jim and Ben approached the buffalo on foot. Rufus was left to guard against anyone or anything that might try and bother the horses.

"Buff have horrible eyesight Ben," he whispered," but they have a sense of smell and hearing that is second to none. Remember that when you are hunting them in the mountains."

They had their long rifles and also Rufus's giving them three quick shots. They left their pistols with Rufus. Two hundred yards from the herd they got down on the hands and knees and crawled until they were seventy-five yards from the herd, then lying on their bellies and using their knees and elbows crawled till they were fifty yards from the buffalo.

"I will take the big bull on the right," Jim whispered. "You take the one on the left. Shoot them eight-ten inches above the front leg. That will place your lead in the heart or lungs."

Ben nodded his head in understanding but wasn't too sure he could hit the side of a barn right now. He had killed Indians, deer and all sorts of small animals and never had he been this nervous. Jim noticed Ben's hands shaking a little and smiled.

"Take two deep breaths and let it our slow." Ben did and most of his shakes went away. Jim took aim and said, "On the count of three. One...two...three. Both rifles fired as one. Jim's dropped in his tracks and Ben's staggered a couple of steps before dropping. Jim had Rufus's rifle and shot a cow. The others slowly ambled away and then the ground started to shake as they began to run.

Jim and Ben stood up and Ben started to walk toward the dead buffalo. "You forgetting something Ben?" Jim asked. Ben looked questionably at Jim and Bill nodded toward the rifle in Ben's hand. "Ben, don't ever and I mean ever fire your rifle and not immediately reload it." He said while reloading his rifle. "It could save your life someday." Advice that Ben never forgot.

James showed up with the pack animals and their mounts. Jim showed them how to skin the one he shot and let them skin the other two. They did a passable job being their first. They fleshed the skins and stretched them out to dry.

"These will make fine coats for us. They butchered the cow and cut the meat in strips, salted it down, and hung the strips to dry out. Rufus started a small fire, and they cooked some steaks from the hump which Jim promised would be downright delicious.

He was not wrong about the steaks. Ben thought they were the best he had ever eaten, but then it could have been the fact the only thing they have eaten since leaving St. Louis was jerky, rabbit and a little venison.

They decided to stay here for a couple days and let the hides dry out in the sun before moving on. Jim said they should be in the foothills of the Rockies in three days or so. This news brought a little excitement in Ben's and Rufus's life that had become somewhat boring the last few days.

Two days later excitement flowed through both young men's veins as they sat on their mounts looking at the blue shrouded mountains fifty or more miles to the west. The distance made no difference to them. They could see where this trail they had been on was going to end. At the end of the day when camp was made, sleep for the two young men was hard to come by. Jim finally had to tell them to shut the hell up so he could go to sleep. He turned on his side, his back to them and smiled. He remembered his first look at the mountains and would remember it till the day he died.

Late the next day the snow on the mountains could be seen by the men. Ben and Rufus were so excited they did not want to stop to make camp. Common sense prevailed when Jim explained to them that maybe they didn't need the rest but their horses damn sure did. He said he didn't think you boys would like the idea of hauling all your supplies not to mention the heavy buffalo robes on their own backs because their mounts and pack horses gave out. They made camp.

Chapter Eight

Ben was not sure what day of April this day was, but he did know it was the best day of his life. He sat on his mount in the foothills of the Rockies looking up at mountains he never knew could be so tall. Some he could not see the tops because they were hidden by clouds. Snow covered a lot of them and looking at the tall pines, well it took his breath away. It was hard for him to believe that he was fixing to live his dream. He looked at Rufus and his smile were as wide as the Missouri River.

While Ben was looking at his friend the smile disappeared and was replaced by one of shock. An arrow was sticking out his chest. Rufus reached and clasped a hand on Bens shoulder and then fell off his horse. Ben, in shock at what happened sat there for an instant before Bill's shout to run brought him to his senses. An arrow cut the air by his head as he looked at the still body of his friend and knowing Rufus was dead kicked his horse hard and followed Bill at a dead run.

From the hill to their right came four Indians running their ponies hard trying to cut them off. Jim reined in hard and Ben did also. Ben drew his long rifle out when he saw Jim drawing his. They took aim at the running Indians that were no more than fifty yards away and coming straight at them releasing arrows. Jim fired and then Ben. Two warriors were flung backwards off their ponies hitting the rocky ground hard and rolling a couple times and lay still. Both men pulled their pistols and at almost point-blank range fired. They both shot the same Indian or one missed and the one remaining warrior left his pony's back and slammed into Ben like a charging buffalo. Both men hit the ground hard with Ben getting the worse of it being on bottom. He was stunned and took a second or two to gain his senses. As he did so he saw the man, who was sitting astride his chest, raise his hand to deliver a killing blow with a tomahawk. Quick reflex saved Ben from certain death as he let loose with a right fist that caught the man square on the point of his chin knocking him off Ben's chest and on his back. Ben rolled and drew his butcher knife and stabbed the stunned man in the chest, pulled it out and stabbed him again.

He stood up and looked around for his pistol and rifle. Finding them he looked at Jim who was slumped over his saddle. Rushing to him He grabbed Jim and lay him gently on the ground. An arrow was in his chest and blood trickled from the corner of his mouth. Ben knew what that meant, a lung had been pierced. Ben shook the man, and his eyes flew open. A groan came from his lips.

Ben laid Jim's head gently on the ground and remembering Jim's words he reloaded his and Jim's rifles and pistols. This saved his life as another Indian, the one whose arrow had hit Jim, charged form the brush not twenty feet away just as Ben finished reloaded the last pistol. The warriors timing could not have been worse as Ben fired the freshly loaded gun and the back of the man's head exploded as the ball passed thru his right eye and out the back of his head.

Grabbing the other pistol Ben dropped to the ground looking around quickly in all directions for more trouble. Five minutes went by with no more Indians. Ben moved quickly to Jim and sat down beside the man and lifting the man's head laid it in his lap. Jim looked up and asked.

"Did we get all of them?"

Ben nodded his head. "I think so."

"Good. Now listen good boy to what I'm telling you. We are in the southernmost part of the foothills of the Rockies. Go to the mountains and turn north for several days till you come to a large river (later called The South Platt) and swing northwest. You will be in the southern part of the Rockies. Just find you some streams that have beaver dams and start trapping.

Jim, now gasping and struggling for words kept talking. "Don't trap all the beaver in any one place. Leave some to repopulate the stream. Work your traps and keep working your way north. You will be in God's country then, deep in the Rockies. At the first sign of cold weather find you a cave and stock it with firewood and food. Take my heavy buffalo coat and with the other hides we have you should be able to make a good blanket and find a use for the other one."

Jim was really struggling now and with every word blood poured out between his lips. When he began choking Ben raised his head up and it helped some.

Jim looked over at the dead Indian. "Comanche," he said. "Others will come looking for their brothers Ben so get the hell away from here and let a man die in peace. I've made my peace with God and I'm not scared of dying."

"Jim, I don't know what to say," Ben said choking on his own words.

"Don't say anything Ben. Just go to them mountains and live a good and free life."

Ben looked down with tears rolling down his cheeks. "Jim, I wi…" he didn't finish as he saw Jim's eyes set and knew his last friend was gone. He wept.

Ben carried him and laid him the shade of a huge cedar. Using his butcher knife, he scraped out a shallow grave and after wrapping Jim in a wool blanket placed him in the shallow hole and spent an hour carrying rocks to cover him to keep the varmints away. He sat there for a few minutes looking at the grave and trying to wrap him mind around what had happened the last few days. He could not get the picture of Rufus's smiling face looking at the Rockies suddenly being wiped out by an arrow and now Jim.

Two weeks or so ago we were some happy, laughing, joking bunch of men. Now there's just me. He looked at the mountains that were only a couple days ride away. *Go to the mountains, turn north till I find a big river then go northwest. Was that what Bill said.* He was trying to remember every word Bill said. At the time he was upset and excited after the fight with the Comanche. Then he remembered something else his friend had said, "Get the hell away from here because their friends will be coming looking for them. He stood up, gathered up Bills weapons and put them on his saddle. He now had three long rifles, three pistols, two butcher knives and his tomahawk. *Quite an arsenal* he thought. He gathered up the horses, his mount and two pack horses. On one of the pack animals he put the heavy buffalo hides and Bill's coat.

On the other he put his and Jims traps which totaled eleven weighing about five pounds each and also his friends possible bag which he put extra lead, powder, paper for wadding and extra flints. He also put about twenty-five pounds of dried buffalo meat. In his saddle bags he had an extra shirt, some powder and lead, cooking utensils, coffee, sugar, and flour. In his possible bag he had flint and steel for making a fire, two bone needles and some thread. He had taken Bills rifle sheath from his dead horse. He now had a rifle on each side of his saddle, a brace of pistols around his waist and one tied to his saddle pommel. He had a butcher knife in his right boot and a tomahawk in his belt on his back and carrying his long gun in is hand. Checking everything again to make sure he had what he needed mounted his horse and leading the pack horses headed toward those snowcapped mountains and toward the unknown.

Two day later he stood beside his mount looking at the scene before and above him. He had traveled most of the night and knew he was close to the mountains when he finally made camp. He was exhausted as was his mounts and pack animals. He slept later than normal and when he awoke the sun was breaking the hills behind him. What he looked at now took his breath away. He had no idea he would be this close to his goal.

Before him loomed snowcapped mountains the like he had never seen. *They must be ten thousand feet tall,* he thought. He stood there staring at the wonder of it all. A plush meadow lay before him and a herd of elk stood looking in his direction no more than three hundred yards away. Two eagles circled overhead and then landed in the top of one of the million pine trees that covered the sides of the mountains for several thousand feet but stopping before reaching the snow-covered peaks. The air was fresh and clean, smelling of pine.

He sat down on a flat rock. *I'm here Rufus. I made it,* his mind wandering, reminiscing of the last month. *Onliest thing that could make this day better would be if you were here seeing this with me.*

And then for really the first time he felt it- loneliness and it hit him hard as he stared at the vastness surrounding him. He was in the mountains he had dreamed of, but he was alone. He had no one to talk to, no one to tell him what direction to go, he was alone. He was in a mountain range that was vast, how vast he did not know but Bill had told him it was hundreds of miles long and two or so hundred miles wide, maybe wider. He was sitting here feeling very small and wondered if there was another white man around. Looking at the elk that were still pretty much ignoring him he figured there wasn't. Then he remembered Jim's dying words

"Travel north till you reach a river then turn northwest and go into the mountains and start trapping working your way north." *Time to forget that you are alone Ben. Time to do what you came here to do. You didn't expect no towns or large crowds of people here so just find a stream and start trapping beaver.*

Chapter Nine

One Month Later

It was late in the afternoon as Ben sat on a stump contemplating thing. A slight breeze brushed his cheeks, an eagle soared high overhead, and the only sound was the creek rushing over rocks before slowing into the deep pool formed by the dam the beavers had built. Two bull elks stood one hundred yards away watching the strange thing sitting by the creek. After a month of trapping and always working his way northwest deeper into the mountains he knew a white man was not seen here before or at least seldom seen.

He had been lucky so far; no Blackfoot or Utes had been seen and no grizzlies. He had seventy pelts and was pretty proud of himself. The only thing he had talked to in over a month was to himself and his horse. His horse wasn't much of a conversationalist but did nod and shake his head every once in a while, making Ben think he agreed or disagreed with whatever he had said. At this rate he would have close to two hundred pelts by the time the rendezvous begin in mid-June at least that is when Bill said it was. Course he had no idea where this was to take place but only hoped he stumbled into another trapper before then.

He had taken five pelts from his traps this morning and they were stretched out on peg drying out. He had baited the traps again and would run them first thing in the morning. Bill was right when he said there was always work to do for a trapper. Setting traps, running the traps, skinning the beaver and stretching the hides, mending clothes, mending traps, and hunting for something to cook and eat made a full day. Of course, there was also the horses to brush and feed also. He had actually, at least to his thinking, had done a first-class job making blankets from the buffalo hides he had carried with him. All in all, when the sun set and after a cup of coffee it was dang nice to stretch out on the soft, thick pine needles that covered the ground and go to sleep. He kept the horses close to him at night as they would let him know with their stomping and whinnying if anything was approaching the camp.

Lying on one of the blankets this night he was startled when his horse whinnied and was staring off into the darkness his ears twitching back and forth. Ben grabbed his Hawken and stood, crouched looking where his horse was staring his thumb on the hammer. A minute passed and he was startled again when a voice cried out, "Hello the camp."

"Who are you?" Ben shouted back.

"Jeb Smith," the man hollered back. "Smelled your coffee thought I might have a cup."

"Come in careful like," Ben warned.

A minute later the man came into view his rifle held over his head with one hand and leading his horse and two pack horses with the other. Ben wondered if this was the Jeb Smith he had read about. *Surely not*, he thought, *because this man was about maybe five eight inches tall and could not weigh more than a hundred and fifty pounds. If this is him, I figured he was over six feet and at least two hundred pounds of muscle from all the stories I had heard and read.*

The man looked at this big, strapping young man, and said. "Don't believe I know you. You new out here?" he said laying his rifle on a stump.

Ben relaxed, and laughed, "About as new as one can get. A greener I believe I would be called.

Looking around the camp and noticing things were as they should be. "Well, I couldn't tell by looking at your camp. Looks like you have done well nodding toward the stack of pelts."

"There's some coffee left so get your cup and have a seat. If I talk too much it's because I haven't seen another white man for over a month. Tired of talking to myself so just put up with me." He was sure it was the

Smith he had read about when the man laid his Bible beside the small fire that he had taken out of his saddle bags when he got his cup. Jeb Smith was a righteous, God loving man besides being one of the most famous of the mountain men. He was known for always reading the Bible.

"How did you make it out here by yourself?" Jeb asked.

Ben went into telling the whole story of the men he was with and what happened leaving nothing out.

Jeb shook his head. "Know'd Jim for mor'n three years, maybe more. He was a good trapper and was upright and honest in his dealings with other trappers. Think he was a religious man too."

Ben said. "He was that. Last words was where he had made his peace with God and he wasn't afraid of dying."

"Good," Jeb said. "So many men out here die and don't know their God or anything about the Bible. How about you Ben, you a believer?'

Ben hesitated for a few seconds before answering. "I believe there is a God who created all this and everything on this earth. I know some about the Bible. Ma used to read it to us a lot. I know that God's son died for our sins and some men followed him around and preached. Also and some man, can't remember his name talked to God on a mountain top and received His Commandments or rules to live by.

Jeb chuckled, "The Apostles."

"Yeah that's them," Ben said smiling.

"And Moses."

"Yes sir that's him" Ben said slapping his leg and laughing.

"Well it's good to know we have another believer in this mountains because Lord knows they are few of us."

"Jim said the trappers got together in June and traded pelts for the things they needed with the fur companies' representatives."

Jeb nodded. "Yep, that would be the rendezvous we have each year." He chuckled, "that's where the fur companies and other merchants get rich and we just get by."

What do you mean by that?"

"The merchants come a long ways to buy and trade for our plews and they charge five times the price for things that you would pay in St Louis. So, by the time a trapper buys new traps, lead, powder, coffee, flour and a hundred other things he needs he is lucky to have any money left over. On a good year after buying supplies a trapper might have a couple hundred dollars left for a year of work. If you are coming here to get rich you've made a big mistake but if you come here for other reasons like the freedom you have and living in the most beautiful place on earth then it's worth it."

"Don't get me wrong about the money. I've had some good years and trappers like Bridger, Coulter, Walker and a few others have done well."

"What is a good number for plews?"

"I'd say the average is about two hundred and fifty to three hundred. I had six hundred last year but that probably won't happen again. I know Bridger had four hundred and fifty, but most had three hundred or a little less. If you can get over three hundred you can make out okay."

"Looks like I will be a little short this year since I just started," Ben said in a somber tone.

"Maybe I can help out some. If you like I can travel north with you and sorter show you around. I think maybe you would have a hard time finding the rendezvous unless you met some other trappers."

Ben attitude brighten up. "I'd more than welcome your company Mr. Smith.

They shook hands. "Name is Jeb, not Mr. Smith." They both laughed.

Chapter Ten

Late May 1825

Four weeks had passed since Ben and Jeb formed a partnership. They had trapped one stream after another always working their way northwest and deeper into the Rockies. Ben had learned a lot from Jeb about life in the mountains. He had honed his tracking and reading sign skills to a new level. Jeb had learned that Ben was one eager beaver to learn everything he needed to know about survival. He practiced his sign language almost every night to the point he was as proficient as Jeb was.

So far, they had seen no Indians and no other white men and best of all, no grizzles. That changed early one morning while they camped on the bank of the South Platte River which they had been following for several days.

As they were breaking camp five Indians came upon their camp. They were as surprised as the two white men. Immediately they cut loose with the war cries and charged the camp.

"Blackfoot," Jeb hollered as he grabbed his long gun and Ben followed suite. Both men fired their rifles at the same time and two warriors were swept off their feet and hit the rocky ground. Jeb pulled one of his pistols and fired almost point blank into the face of another the ball entering the forehead of the Blackfoot killing him instantly.

Ben had not picked up his pistols which still lay on his bedroll. A warrior slammed into him, both hitting the ground hard. Ben was up quickly as was the brave and both pulled their knives and squared off facing each other. Ben studied the man's face and figured he was middle age and was probably a hand at knife fighting. They circled for a few seconds then the Indian took a quick step toward Ben and slashed at Ben's stomach hoping to gut him like one would a deer. Ben stepped back quickly, and the blade missed by a whisker.

Ben swung a vicious left at the Blackfoot's chin and connected solidly knocking the man out. Ben turned and saw Jeb fighting with the fifth warrior. The warrior straddled Jeb's chest and was preparing to bash his head with a war club when Ben hit the man like a battering ram and knocked him off his friend and slashed with his butcher knife its razor sharp blade cutting deep into the warrior's throat. The Indian dropped his club and while on his knees grabbed his throat with both hands, blood gushing out his mouth and between his fingers. Black eyes stared for a couple seconds at Ben who could feel the hate flowing from them. A second later the man fell forward his face smashing into the hard-rocky ground.

Ben turned at the crack of a pistol and saw the brave he had struck a moment before tumbling to the ground. He had ducked and hit the ground rolling just as Jeb had pulled the trigger the ball missing its mark and smashing into the trunk of a large pine.

The warrior was up immediately and charged Ben howling a hideous war cry from his throat and banishing a butcher knife. Ben whirled to face his attacker and grabbed the man's arm holding the knife that had begun to arc toward his body. Grabbing the arm just above the wrist Ben held on with a vice like grip and plunged his knife upwards towards the man stomach. It was stopped suddenly by a hand that squeezed his wrist so tightly he could not break it loose.

They stayed in that position for a few seconds and then Ben realized he was losing his grip on the man's sweaty arm and knew it was now or never. He fell backwards toward the ground and pulled the surprised Indian with him. As he was falling he raised his right foot and placed it in the man's belly and when the warrior was above him he kicked out with his foot with all his strength and released his hold on the man's wrist at the same time throwing the man high in the air and doing a flip in the air. He hit hard on the back of his neck and shoulder and Ben was on him quicker than you could spit driving his knife to the hilt in the Blackfoot's chest. Ben collapsed exhausted by the struggle.

"You are going to be something in these here mountains," Jeb said sweeping his left arm upward and in a circle toward the mountains. "Killing that man,'" nodding toward the warrior who Ben had just killed with the knife, "was no small feat. I know who he is." He paused a moment taking a swallow of water from his canteen. "He is Running Fox, one of the greatest of the Blackfoot warriors. He has counted many coup including my old partner who he killed two years ago with a knife." He reached out his hand and shook Bens. "Thanks for avenging him."

"How can you be sure it was him?"

"There were ten of us in the party that day. There was my partner, Ben Williams, good friends, Jeremy Taylor, Will Smith, and six other trappers I knew but not real well. We were headed to the rendezvous when we rode into an ambush." He hesitated not really wanting to talk about it but wanted Ben to know what he had done.

"Jeremy and myself were in the front of the group when the attack started. They were all around us and arrows filled the air. We all followed Jeremy to the right where there were some huge rocks that we could get behind and fight. We all made it except Will who had three arrows in his chest. His horse was killed, and three other horses had to be put down after the fight that had arrows in them. We all opened up with our long rifles and all being trappers for a few years we all had been through this before and no one panicked. Our fire was accurate, and several Blackfoot went down immediately. We fired our pistols and several more fell then they were on us like a pack of hungry wolves swinging war clubs and knives. I managed to kill the one that was on me and I turned to where Ben was and saw this Blackfoot bury his knife in Ben's chest. I drew my second pistol and shot at him, but he turned just as I stroked the trigger and I hit him in the back of the left shoulder."

"He looked over his shoulder at me and I saw his face clearly and will never forget it. Anyway, we fought them off and had one prisoner who was severely wounded. We lost Ben and Will, and a man named James Fenton. Two more of our group was wounded but neither was life threatening." He walked over to the body and taking his knife slit the back and pulled the deer skin shirt back to reveal an ugly scar on the back of his left shoulder. "That good enough proof," he asked looking at Ben?

Jeb took another drink before continuing. The one that was wounded we tried to get information from him. I speak enough Blackfoot lingo to communicate with him. We wanted to know if there was a main party somewhere close and how many. We wanted to know why they attacked us because at that time we not having much trouble with the Blackfoot like we are now: The Bloods and the Utes, yes but not the Blackfoot. Later we found out the Blackfoot along with the Kainai or Bloods and the Northern Piegans had formed a federation and were committed to killing all the trappers in the mountains. They felt like we were killing the game that they needed to feed their families plus just resenting our presence in their domain."

"Shoot man, they made war on the Shoshones, the Flatheads, the Crow, the Sioux and any other tribe that entered their domain. Anyone that was not a Blood, Piegans, or Blackfoot was an enemy and was to be killed without mercy. Double that for the white trappers who each knew they had not better be taken alive. Remember that Ben: do not be taken alive and expect mercy because it's not in their vocabulary. I know the Good Book says do not ever take your own life because life is precious but, in some cases, as in this, I think God would understand."

'Anyway," Jeb continued to get back to where I found out Running Fox's name. The only information we got out the captured Blackfoot before he died was the man who I had wounded was named Running Fox and he was a war chief. In case you didn't know one does not become a war chief because he wants to; he earns it in battle by being braver than anyone else and killing more of his enemies than anyone else. That was no ordinary brave you killed my friend. I intend to spread the word at the rendezvous about your killing him and a lot of men there will want to thank you for it. We've all lost friends at his hand the last two years."

A week had passed since the encounter with Running Fox and his party with no more sightings of any Indians. Things were normal with trapping and moving every two or three days. Beaver were plentiful and Ben was doing okay. He found out three weeks ago he had a long way to go to be a successful trapper though. Jeb had almost twice as many plews as he did. Jed had given him basic instructions but did not go with him when they set and run their traps.

Ben had about a hundred seventy-five plews and Jed had well over two hundred and fifty and Ben already had about seventy when they met.

This day began as the previous day and the one before that and the one before that. They ran their traps with Jeb going downstream and Ben upstream. Ben was excited as he had seven beaver in his eleven traps. He was finishing re-setting his last trap when he heard a low growl behind him. Whirling around he saw the grizzly about thirty yards from him. The beast stood on his hind legs sniffing the air trying to figure out what it was he smelled. "*Damn,*" been thought, *He must be ten foot tall. Stand still and don't make a sound,* he said to himself. He was scared, really scared and wasn't sure he could have moved even if he wanted to. The bear stood there a full thirty seconds sniffing and growling before dropping to all fours and to Ben's relief headed back into the woods. Ben stood there a full five minutes before he picked up three of the beaver and headed back to camp. He had his hands full as an adult beaver weighed thirty to fifty pounds. The three plus his rifle made a hefty weight to carry. He would come back for the other four he had trapped.

Jeb was in camp when he arrived, and he quickly recounted the run in with the grizzly. Jed stood there with his long rifle's butt on the ground and his palms on the end of the barrel and his chin on top of his hands.

"You were fortunate Ben, very fortunate. Apparently, the bear had not smelled a human before and didn't know what your smell was. Probably a female because an old male would have investigated to see what the smell was and you would be his lunch by now." He chuckled, "Luck was with you today, but you did the right thing in not moving or shooting. You would have only infuriated him or her and would have charged. Remember this because you more than likely will have other encounters: your lead ball unless you are really lucky will not penetrate the skull so try to hit him square in the chest if he is standing or behind his front leg for a lung shot. Course that's hard to do if he is charging straight at you."

So, what do I do then?"

"Prepare to meet your maker."

Chapter Eleven

The sun had not broken over the mountains when after a quick breakfast and coffee Jeb said his goodbyes to Ben. The night before he had explained to Ben, he had promised a friend he would meet him three days from now and were going to look for a passage west thru the mountains. He hoped Ben had learned a few things from him and wished him luck and would see him at the rendezvous. He had given the young man specific directions as to where the rendezvous would be and when.

In the last few weeks Ben had developed a sense of direction that the trappers had to have to find their way through the mountains and arriving where they were supposed to be. He was no way the greenhorn he was two months ago, but them again he was nowhere an accomplished trapper like Jeb Smith was. *Yep, I feel good about myself, but I know I have a long ways to go in learning all there is to know about surviving in these beautiful mountains. Maybe a man will never know all the ways because there is just so many ways a man can die out here.* He thought a moment. *But God knows I love it.*

He walked over to where Jeb sat on his horse reaching up to take Jed's offered hand.

"Thanks for everything Jeb."

"You're welcome "greener"," he said laughing. "Watch your back and I'll see you at the rendezvous." He turned his horse and trotted off then turning in the saddle and looking back at Ben over his shoulder said, "Keep that long black hair on your head and not on a Blackfoot's lance." He laughed again and was gone.

Ben watched till he was out of sight and sat on a large flat rock and when looking at the sky, the vast mountains all around him it hit him like a fist to the stomach: He was alone again. He immediately walked over to his saddlebags and took out a piece of paper and a pencil scribbling down the directions exactly as Jeb had given him so he would not forget one word of information.

He began taking inventory of his food, traps, weapons, powder and lead. He had two long rifles and two pistols, little over a pound of lead, his bullet mold, two pounds of powder, his tomahawk and two butcher knives as well as a skinning knife. In his possible bag he had a cache of about twenty lead balls, extra flint for his rifles and pistols, needle, some thread, flint and metal striker for staring fires, and other miscellaneous items. He had eleven traps, almost 200 beaver plews, five pounds of coffee, about fifteen pounds of dried buffalo strips, some sugar and salt and a little flour. He had a half pound of powder in his buffalo horn that hung around his neck. He had a coat from a buffalo and two blankets from the hides as well as a couple wool ones. As far as clothes was concerned, he had a pair of extra moccasins, a wool shirt and a pair of fur lined gloves.

After taking inventory he squatted by the fire and drank the last cup of coffee that was in the pot he and Jed had been drinking. Well, one thing for sure is that I am well armed and have plenty of lead and powder, at least enough to hold me till the rendezvous. Food should be no problem with what I have and can kill. Finishing his coffee, he rinsed the pot and the cup and put them in his saddle bags with the food stuff he had. Gathering up his traps, coat, blankets and other things he tied them on the back of one of the pack horses. He had his plews bundled and on the backs of the other two horses. He saddled his horse and after tying the saddle bags on behind he mounted and after a quick look around to make sure he not forgotten anything he headed north to the next stream.

Over the next week he had placed his traps in two streams but only had four more plews to show for his efforts. His traps had been sprung but no beaver. He could find no tracks on the bank showing an animal had taken them. He was at a loss as to what was happening to them. Some of the traps had been placed on dry land after being taken from the water. He figured he should have had twenty or twenty-five plews instead of four.

It's not an animal at least not the four-legged kind. He didn't want to think it could be another trapper running his traps but what else could it be. He squatted by the fire drinking a cup of coffee. It was a beautiful morning, the sun just making its self-shown over the tops over the mountains. He had already set his traps and would run them again this afternoon.

I think I will stay up tonight and watch some of the traps and see what I can find out what's happening. He threw the contents of the cup in the fire causing ashes to fly and a lot of smoke which he immediately wished he had not done that. He checked the horses and then lay down on his blanket to catch a little sleep. *May be a long night,* he thought.

He fell asleep immediately. A hidden figure watched the camp from the pine tree about a hundred yards away. He was watching the camp with a spyglass he had acquired when he was a sailor on a merchant ship that was in the hide and talon trade. He was on the ship for two years before he had had enough of long days, hard work, and poor food.

Jeremy Sledge was twenty-eight years old and plenty tough. He was six foot in his stocking feet and weighed one hundred-eighty pounds of muscle. Two years of seamanship and continually brawling at the ports had left him more than confident of being able to take of himself. He had been a good seaman, well thought of by the ship's captain but a total failure as a trapper. He had though, been a very successful thief running other trapper's lines which he found much easier than working his butt off and nothing to show for it.

The man he was watching was young, very young compared to the other trappers he had watched and robbed. He also saw that he was a very big young man and was pretty good at what he was doing. As he watched the man lay down on his blanket. *What is he doing lying down at this time of day,* he wondered? Then it came to him and he smiled. *He knows someone or something is running his traps so he's snoozing now and going to stay up tonight watching.* Jeremy backed carefully away from the camp and made his way the half mile to his camp to wait till night.

Midnight found Ben a quarter mile from camp and watching three of his traps from behind a deadfall of an old pine tree that that had been a victim of a lightning strike. So far he had seen nothing but a couple of coons and some elk than came to the stream for a drink.

Meanwhile, back at his camp Jeremy was looking at one of Ben's stack of plews. Damn, this young'un has done pretty good for himself he thought as he struggles to pick up a bundle that must have weighed over one hundred and fifty pounds. He managed to get it over his shoulder and carried it out of camp to where he had picketed his horse about one hundred yards away.

He was headed back for another bundle when he saw the youngster coming back by the light of a full moon. He backed away quietly and watched.

Ben, being pretty frustrated that he had seen nothing bothering his traps walked directly to the fire and picking up his tin cup on the rock beside the still hot coals of his campfire poured what remained of the coffee in the pot into his cup. He picked up a stick and stirred the coals and small flame appeared. Ben added a couple sticks to the small fire.

Upset that he had no more idea of what was happening to his traps than he did before he did not notice that one of his three bundles was missing as he sipped the coffee. After a few minutes he threw the remainder of his coffee into the fire and lay down on his blanket to get some rest before running his traps at first light.

Chapter Twelve

The next morning things were back to normal: Ben had five beavers in his traps and the rest of the traps had not been sprung. He figured it was time to move again since he did not want to trap every beaver here.

He skinned the five he had and rolled the pelts up tightly and bound each with rawhide to keep till the next camp where he could flesh them and stake them out to dry. Gathering things up and placing them on the horses so he could leave. He suddenly realized he was missing a bundle of plews.

"What the hell" he exclaimed loudly. Quickly looking around he searched for the missing bundle. Realizing it was gone, a month's worth of work, he frantically searched for clues that would tell him what had happened.

Carefully studying the ground, he found the tracks of a man, a man whose tracks were smaller than his. He followed them where they left the camp and noticed they were much deeper than the ones coming into camp. "Carrying my damn plews on his shoulder when he left."

He said out loud. He followed the tracks to where the man's horse was tied and then on to his camp which was empty. He felt of the coals which were cold. *Been gone for hours,* he thought to himself. He looked around looking for something, anything that might give him some hope of who this man was. The only clue he had come from the tracks of one of his pack animals. Its left front hoof turned in abnormally. "I'll remember you, you son-of-a-bitch," he muttered. "I'll remember."

He made his way back to his camp and after checking again for anything not packed, he headed north to the next stream. He was glad now that most of his plews had his initials on the underside which he put burned there with a burning stick. *If this little man shows up with that pack animal at the rendezvous, I'll have my fun.*

Midafternoon found Ben camped beside a small stream. He had scouted the stream and found three dams on it indicating beaver. He took the five plews he had rolled up and using a small knife started removing the flesh from the underside of each and then stretching them out and staking them on the ground to dry.

He left camp and set out his traps. Returning, he took some rope and threw it over a stout limb of a pine about ten feet off the ground. Tying the rope to a bundle he them hoisted each off the ground and tied the rope to the tree making sure it was not easy to see. With each bundle over ten foot off the ground he felt fairly certain they were safe.

That done he prepared himself a meal of biscuits and jerky not wanting to start a fire that might give his location away. He sat leaning back on a log and chewed his food watching, ever alert to thing going on around him. This saved his life.

The twang of an arrow being launched from a bow reached his ears and instantly he rolled to his left pulling his pistol as he did. An instant later the arrow stuck in the log where he had been. He came up on one knee in time to see an Indian about twenty yards away with his arm above his head fixing to launch an eight-foot-long spear. Hastily aiming Ben triggered the pistol and the heavy ball caught the brave dead center of the chest. He dropped the spear and looked down at the bloody hole in his chest, looked at Ben and then fell face forward striking the ground hard.

The sound of running feet got his attention to his right and looking he saw another Indian charging him with a tomahawk raised ready to bash in this white man's head. Ben, quickly standing to meet this challenge drew his tomahawk and prepared to meet the warrior.

Ben quickly noticed this warrior was no youngster and was larger than most he had seen. The brave swung his tomahawk in a downward angle intended to bash the white man's head. Ben was already stepping back and the razor-sharp blade missed its target but the running momentum of the Indian resulted in him crashing into Ben with both falling to the ground. Ben was up instantly, and the warrior was just as quick even though both had been stunned when hitting the hard ground.

Ben stepped back again as the blade of the tomahawk just missing his stomach. Now, both men circled to their right feigning with their weapons, studying the reaction of their opponent with each move looking for a weakness.

The Indian made a sweeping swing again at his stomach and stepping back he let the blade pass and before the man could bring his weapon back Ben stepped in close and sent a terrible blow to the man's cheek with his left fist. Staggered by the blow Ben's opponent was vulnerable, and Ben swung his tomahawk at a forty-five degree angle and caught the warrior in the neck almost severing the man's head. The man stood for almost five seconds even though he was dead before falling to the ground.

Ben made a quick search of the area and found their ponies. *Thank God there were only two and no one got away,* he thought.

He was startled by a clap of thunder and looked at the top of the mountains to the west. "Damn," he cursed as he looked at the ugly dark clouds that hid the tops of the mountains and moving fast toward him.

He quickly moved the bodies of the two Indians away from his camp. He picketed his horses as well as hobbling them so they could not go far if they pulled loose when the storm hit. He stowed his pelts and other gear under the limbs of a huge pine and pulled his buffalo blanket from the back of his horse. He quickly unsaddled the horse and put the saddle and saddle bags away just as the wind picked up and the first drops of rain began falling.

He sat down away from the trees and near the horses not wanting to be near one if lightning struck. Wrapping the blanket around his body and head he waited. He did not to have to wait long as the storm struck suddenly. Wind tried to rip the blanket from him, and the rain came so hard that he could not even see his horses when he peeked through the fold of the blanket.

It was over in a few minutes. He unwrapped himself from the blanket and looking around saw his three horses were standing where he picketed and shaking their bodies and heads trying to shake the cold water off.

Outside of being soaked everything seemed to be okay. He decided it best if he moved into the trees and built a fire to dry things out otherwise with wet bedding it would be a chilly night.

The sun appeared as the clouds passed and the warming rays were bringing warmth back into his body as well as the horses. He spread his blanket on the rocky ground away from the pines to dry the hair as well as the heavy coat. He made coffee and squatted by the fire feeling its warmth.

Looking around he suddenly cursed. "Damnation," he shouted causing his horses to turn their heads and look at him. He just realized that with the heavy rain any idea of going back and tracking the man who stole his plews would be impossible. The only good thing was he had learned a valuable lesson: he would never leave camp again unless his plews and other essentials were hidden.

One good thing came from the rain, the men he had killed tracks would have been wiped out also. He was thankful he had not turned their ponies loose because they would have surely eventually made it back to where they had come from and would be easy to track in the wet ground back here.

He looked at his blanket and coat where the warming rays from the sun was resulting in steam rising from them as they dried. I'll spend the rest of the day here while things are drying out and then move a couple miles upstream before making camp. He left to gather his traps so he would be ready to move. He hid his plews under some broken limbs and left to retrieve his traps.

Two hours later he was back in camp with his traps. He looked up at the sun's position in the sky and figured it to be around four o'clock. Walking over to where he had hidden the plews and other essentials he was surprised to find them almost dry, at least on the outside. He untied the rope that he had tied bound them with and looked at the second plew. He was elated when he found it dry as old piece of desert wood. "The old hides are almost waterproof," he chuckled. He walked over to his where his blanket and coat was staked out. They were not completely dry but were close to being usable and wearable. *They will be by nightfall,* he thought.

He gathered some rocks and formed a circle to build a small fire. He took his flint and steel striker out of his possible bag. He took a small piece of cloth from his bag also that he kept for this reason: damp grass and twigs that would make starting a fire harder to do. Using his striker, he hit the flint with it causing sparks which soon ignited the cloth and small twigs he had gathered along with bigger pieces of wood. The twigs caught finally and when they were all burning, he added a couple pieces of the larger limbs. Finally, when there was only coals he placed his coffee pot on them and waited for the water to get hot.

Sipping the hot coffee, he squatted by the rocks surrounding the coals and thought about things. *It's almost time for the rendezvous and I don't have any idea if I'm close to the Green River area or not. In fact, ole boy, you don't have any dang idea where you are except in the mountains.* He chuckled, *this one hell of a fix you are in. Got plews, probably going to get more and may not find the meeting place to sell them which is going to put me in a hell of a fix with not being able to buy supplies for the winter.* "Damn!" he cursed loudly. The horses raised their heads and looked at him for a second and then went back to chomping the grass.

He really didn't know what to do for the first time. He knew he had followed the directions his dying friend and Jeb had given him so he must be close...but how close or how far he did not have a clue. He refilled his cup after taking the paper out of the possible bag he had written the directions the best he could remember on. Reading them again and then again, he felt he had to be close.

He stood up and walked to where his blanket and coat were. Both were dry and he slipped the coat on as the sun was dipping behind the mountain tops and the temperature would be falling quickly as darkness set in. He brought the horses in closer to him and picketed them as well as putting hobbles on them. He spread the blanket on the ground and brought his saddle over to use as a pillow. He checked the camp again to make sure everything is as should be and then lay down on the blanket and looking up, stared at the stars that were beginning to show themselves.

He did not know how he had been asleep when the whinny of one of the horses woke him. He lay still for a couple seconds trying to get focused where he was and what had suddenly woken him. He glanced at the horses and one nickered again and all were looking into the trees toward the south, their ears twitching. Rolling slowly onto his left side he looked in the direction they were looking but saw nothing. He knew to trust a horse's sense of smell or hearing when something or someone was near. Sitting up slowly he thrust his pistols in his belt and also his tomahawk. His butcher knife was in his right moccasin boot. Picking up his long rifle he stood up and put a hand on the nearest horse.

"Easy boy," he whispered. "Easy". He stoked the horse's neck while never taking his eyes off the tree line. The half-moon was low in the sky but still cast enough light that he could see fairly well but in a short while it was going to be dark as sin just before first light.

His heart was beating fast, his breath came a lot faster than normal, and he realized he was shaking a little. He took a deep breath and let it out slowly. *Relax, calm yourself,* he thought to himself. *Relax.* He was ready, calmer now and thinking clearly. *Could be that trapper thief followed me figuring I was easy.* He thought some more while his eyes never quit moving, searching. *Could be Indians that followed me from where I killed their friends. Could be nothing,* but he knew better. *Something or someone was watching him.*

Five minutes passed, then ten, and the first faint light of the new day was making its presence known. With that first light Ben was looking at two Indians whose bodies blended in with brush and trees and one was letting loose an arrow as he looked.

Chapter Thirteen

Ben, seeing this twisted is body against the horse but the arrow, intended for his chest hit him in the left arm just above the elbow. Grimacing with the sudden pain he dropped to one knee and felt the air spit by another arrow passing from the other warrior that just missed his head. He pulled one of the pistols and quickly aiming at the nearest brave feathered the trigger. A flash of smoke was followed by the explosion as the lead ball split the early morning air and found its target. The nearest brave was catapulted backwards as the heavy ball hit him in square in the middle of his chest exploding his heart and leaving a hole in his back one could put his fist through.

Quickly looking where, the other one was he saw nothing...he had disappeared. Ben quickly moved among the horses so not to make himself an easy target. His eyes were desperately searching the trees because in a situation like this the advantage belonged to the hunter, him knowing where his prey was and the prey not knowing where he was.

His arm was hurting something fierce, but there was no time to look at it now. He was on one knee under a horse with the others moving back and forth on the picket lines which gave him some sort of protection. He quickly reloaded the pistol he had discharged and waited. He was waiting, watching and moving some not staying in one spot for than a few seconds among the horses.

The early morning air was heavy and cool, but Ben was sweating like he was in the middle of a desert in July. Nothing moved, even the horses had calmed down and were standing still with their heads up which told Ben he still had company. He knew of one but were there more?

Suddenly the horses moved past him and pulled on their picket stakes. Ben whirled around just in time to see a brave four steps away with a tomahawk raised and would be able to smash his skull in two more steps. Forgetting the pain in his arm Ben, who had been holding his Hawken in his left hand swung his arm up and the blade of the tomahawk glanced off the Hawken. Ben fired his pistol into the belly of the warrior and the man was knocked backwards several feet, stood there slightly bent over looking at this white man who had just killed him before falling face down on the rocky ground.

He did not have time to relish his still being alive as the blood curdling scream from another warrior cause him to whirl around. He saw another Indian coming at him. He was a big man, chest and arms bulging with muscle unlike most Indians who were slender built. He was an older warrior and had an imprint of a yellow hand painted on the side of his face.

Ben had no time to pull his other pistol as he barely dodged under a sweeping blow from the Indians butcher knife. Missing the white man infuriated the brave and immediately bellowed out his war cry and attacked again. All Ben could do was move backwards dodging the razor sharp blade but did manage to pull his butcher knife from the top of his right moccasin boot and retaliated with a swipe of his own that drew blood from the man's upper thigh. He held his Hawken in his left hand, but the arrow made his arm useless.

Ben saw the look of surprise in the man's eyes at being cut then quickly he saw the hate burning in them as the man increased his attack. Ben knew he had to do something quick because his left arm was useless as the strength in it was fading quickly. Dropping his knife, he grabbed the Hawken in his right hand.

He swung the heavy Hawken's barrel at the leg of the man catching him just below the knee and knocking his leg from under him and when he crumpled Ben, grabbing up his knife buried the knife's ten inch blade between the neck and shoulder blade, withdrew it and buried it again in the man's back. The brave never made a sound as he died.

He spun around again as he heard another warrior charging him but was shocked when the brave fell forward face down in the dirt and then the sound of a long gun reached his ears.

Looking past the Indian he saw three trappers and then saw one had kneeled and fired his long gun.

Walking out to meet them and thank them for saving his life he saw his friend Jeb Stewart standing there smiling.

"How you doing greener," he said laughing and shaking Ben's hand.

"Doing fine now Jeb. Thanks for saving my sorry hide.

One of the other men spoke up. "Looks like you didn't need much help," looking at the three dead braves.

Jeb chuckled. "Men, this here is Ben Watkins, the greener I was telling you about. Ben shook their hands as Jeb introduced each, Pete Biggers and George Curry.

The man who had not said anything yet, George Curry, said "Looks like you did a mite good for a greener," and all laughed.

"Let's see what we can do about that arrow in your arm," Jeb said.

In all the excitement of the fight and with his adrenalin flowing Ben had not paid that much attention to the pain in his arm, but now it hurt like hell. It was going to get worse.

Jeb picked up a small stick. "Bite down on this when I pull it out."

Ben nodded and placed the piece of wood between his teeth. Jeb cut the shaft off about one inch above the skin with his butcher knife.

"Ben, I am going to count to three and pull it thru. Are you ready?" Ben nodded again. Jeb starting counting, "One...two." He jerked the shaft through cleanly before Ben realized it. It hurt like the dickens, but the arm immediately felt better.

Ben spit the piece of wood out not realizing he had bitten it into. "That wasn't too bad."

The man named Biggers chuckled, "Wal thar greener yur shu nuff handled that purty damn wal but let's see how you do this." He lifted his butcher knife from the coals with its blade glowing red.

"Wh..What yu..yu going to do with that," Ben said stuttering his words and his voice quivering.

"Those holes have to be sealed Ben in order to stop the bleeding and keep the chance of infection down. It's going to hurt like all get out, but it has to be done," he said squatting in front of Ben and looking into his eyes. "It has to be done son."

Ben nodded and took a deep breath and held it. When Biggers touched the skin, he moved the blade over the hole. The smell of burned and melted skin was strong. Ben blew out his breath and took another as Biggers closed the hole where the shaft came out.

Ben blew out his breath again and took another. He thought he was going to pass out, but he only swayed back and forth a few times and then opened his eyes. He saw three men staring at him and grinning.

"What the hell you three varmints grinning about. I just went thru some pretty good pain that you induced looking at Biggers...and ya'll are grinning."

George Curry spoke up. "Hell we ain't laughing at you boy, we just impressed how well you handled it. Most men pass out when the blade is used. You did good boy."

"Better than you did Biggers when we sealed that knife wound you had in your shoulder." Jeb chuckled, "You passed plum out."

"Wal let me tll yu somthang preacher man. I aint ever had no pain like that. I ain't afraid of ole Lucfer his own damn self but..." He stopped when he saw they were laughing at him and realized they were just funning him. He looked at Ben who was laughing. "Wal yu shore nuff know whut it feels like." Ben nodded his agreement and grimaced.

Jeb looked at Biggers and Curry. "Let get our stuff off the horses. We"ll stay here a couple days to let Ben heal up some."

Later, sitting around the small fire sipping coffee and enjoying the company Ben asked. "Jeb, I thought when you left you were meeting a friend to find a passage through the mountains?"

"Never showed up. Don't know whether he was killed or just changed his mind. I was waiting on him when these two showed up. We've known each other for three or four years. That's the thing up here Ben, not that many of us and most go to the rendezvous each year and renew friendships and miss the ones that didn't make it. Dang Utes and Blackfoot are making the number that don't make it more each year."

"Which reminds me," Biggers said. "You knew old Henry Bates didn't you."

"Yeah we trapped together one year. Good man."

"We come cross his body bout two months ago, scalped and cut sumthang feerce. Figgr'd he was done tortur'd a lot afore they kilt him."

Jeb picked up his Bible, stood up and walked over to the horses. He stood by his horse and placed his arms across the horses back and bowed his head saying a few words about his friend to his God before coming back to the fire. Ben refilled Jeb's cup.

Nothing was said for a few minutes until Jeb spoke up. "Trouble with these mountains is that they take a lot of friends from a man. I hate that fact but even with that I love them and the freedom it gives a man who makes them his home. Biggers, you and Curry there know what I am talking about. Ben, I think you will come to loving them and this thing known as freedom too in time."

Ben nodded his head. "I'm learning that already Jeb. I know I'm just a greener, but I know I have what it takes to make them my home: at least I hope I do."

"Wal thar yungun," Biggers said in his weird way of talking. "Frum whut I have see'd frum yu I don't thank yu will have no problem, no sir, no problem at all making it out heer in these heer mowtans."

Jeb laughed and said, "What this old fool is trying to say is that you have the "Hair of the Bear" which is about the highest praise that a trapper can receive from other trappers.

"I appreciate those words Biggers. I hope I can live up to them."

Chapter Fourteen

First Rendezvous 1825

Two days had passed, and Ben's arm was much better. It still pained him some, but he was able to do what he had to do with just some discomfort but not enough he could not handle. He would be in trouble if a dang Blackfoot or Ute decided to challenge him to a fight but otherwise, he could handle his traps, saddle his horse and the other things that needed to be done.

Before Jeb and his friends left he had given Ben more directions to where the rendezvous was taking place in about a week. Ben figured if he cut down on his time spent trapping, he could make it. He thought he had enough plews to buy enough supplies to make it another year but would have little money if any left over.

The next few days were uneventful with Ben taking a few more plews out of a creek last night. He had one hundred forty-five plews to sell. *Would have been nice if I had the fifty that bastard stole, he thought to himself.*

Afew days later one afternoon as he made his way through the woods, he begin to hear music and singing. A few minutes later the forest opened up and before him was the Green River and a hell of lot of people. He was looking at wagons, trappers, and a lot of Indians all mingling together. A banjo could be heard from the midst and he could see men dancing-with other men. He saw no women other than Indian women, so he figured that was why men were having to dance with men just to have a good time.

As he walked into the camp men nodded their heads at him and he returned the nods. Not really knowing what to do or where to put his horses, traps, plews and camping gear he just wandered around taking in the sight.

There were probably seventy-five to a hundred trappers and twice that many Indians. There would be more later There were six wagons which he quickly saw were the traders buying the plews and selling their goods. There were several more wagons just outside of camp which he figured were to carry all the plews back to St Louis or wherever they came from.

Whiskey was everywhere and a lot of the men were drunk, but all seemed to be having a good time. One trapper came up to him and stuck out his hand.

"Jim Bass is the name. Don't know as I know you." He said shaking Ben's hand.

"Ben Watkins," Ben answered, "And this is my first rendezvous.

"Little light on plews ain't you," the man said.

"Had some trouble a couple weeks ago. Came back into my camp from running my traps and a whole bundle, maybe fifty plews was missing. I tracked the man until a damn rainstorm wiped out his tracks. My plews were marked and I will recognize his horses tracks if I see them."

If'n you find him let some the trappers know. We don't tolerate stealing from other trappers and he will answer to trapper's law. Good to meet you Ben. Have a good time. Take your plews to that wagon," he said pointing with his Hawken. "They are the most honest ones here to deal with."

"Thanks Jim," said as the man walked off. He found a place to picket his horses and took the saddle off his horse and the plews and gear off the two pack horses. Taking his Hawken, he strolled over to the wagon Jim had pointed out. He passed one wagon where two trappers were going back and forth with a man about the prices they were paying. He overheard three dollars was being argued over.

He arrived at the wagon Jim had pointed out and found out they were paying three fifty to four dollars depending on the condition of the pelts. He walked back to his camp and loaded his pelts on a pack horse and made his way back to the wagon.

Bill, he didn't catch his last name, was the man doing the buying and trading. He inspected Ben's plews and found them to be in excellent condition.

"How many," he asked.

"One hundred forty-five," Ben replied.

"With the condition these are in I wish you had more."

"Had more but a damn thief got into my camp while I was running my traps and stole a bundle of fifty."

"Too bad", he said. "Tell you what Ben. I will give you," he looked around to see if anyone was listening. "I'll give you four-twenty-five for each pelt. I think that will be the best price you will get. That's roughly six hundred or so dollars if you will trade with me."

Ben, recalling the three dollars he had heard earlier shook the man's hand and they begin counting the plews. When through counting, Ben had more than he had figured, one hundred and fifty-eight which figured out to be about six hundred and seventy dollars.

Ben bought all the supplies he figured he needed: coffee, sugar, flour, thread and needle, lead and powder, a new wool blanket, rope, two new traps, flint, two wool shirts and a pair of wool trousers. He also got a new coffee pot and a tin cup that was big enough to hold a lot of coffee or maybe stew. He also bought a canvas tarp he could wrap his gear in or string it up during a rain. He still had a little money left over if he found out he needed something else. He was a happy fellow. *Next year I'll have twice as many pelts or more and will start making a little money to save,* he thought to himself.

After stowing away his new supplies he wandered around the camp. He came to where a group of men were in a circle whooping and hollering watching two men wrestle. When a man won, he walked to a man in a huge wide brimmed hat. The man handed him some money

Ben asked a man about the money and the man looked at him noticing his size.

"A youngun' like you could win sum money if'n he wanted to that is."

"Win money. How?" Ben asked.

"Pay a dollar to that thar man in the big hat and he will set yu up a match. Yu win he pays yu part of whut he collected."

Ben walked over to the man and paid him a dollar. Twenty minutes later his name was called and walked into the circle of men. Also walking in was a man a little taller than Ben but not quite as heavy. He took off his buckskin shirt and Ben saw there was not an ounce of fat on him. Ben took his off and a few comments was passed around about his bulging muscles and the betting began.

The man Ben spoke with earlier walked over to him.

"That thar is Big Jack Mellows. Ain't ever been beat. Yu luk like yu can handled yur self so I'm betting on yu."

"Thanks," Ben said not taking his eyes off Big Jack. He did not know that the man he was talking to bet a dollar on Big Jack also.

A man in the center of the ring motioned both men to the center with him. He was obviously a little drunk and his breath would catch fire if someone held a lucifer to it.

No gouging of the eyes and no knees to the privates. Other than that, no rules. Fight till one man pats out." He motioned for the two big men to come together.

They circled each other like two big cats each feinting to see the others reaction. Suddenly Big Jack came at Ben like a battering ram. Ben stepped aside and as the man rushed past where he had been Ben tripped him and Jack in the ground hard, face first. Ben stepped back while Jack got back to his feet. A few of the men laughed but shut up when Big Jack glared at them.

Big Jack was little more wary of this youngster now as they moved in a circle again. Unknown to Ben, Jack held a handful of dirt he picked up when he was on the ground. He feinted with his left arm then threw the dirt in Ben's eyes with his right and charged at the same time. Ben was struggling to clear the dirt from his eyes when Jack rammed into him like a bull buffalo. Still not seeing very clear Ben felt his breath leave him when he hit the ground and then felt Jack's weight on him pinning him to the ground as the man straddled his chest. Big mistake. Even though he could not see clearly, he instinctively threw his legs up and scissoring them around Jacks neck he brought them down with all his might and Jack came with them flipping like a rag doll.

His eyes were watering but he began to see clearly as the tears washed the dirt away. He quickly rushed to where Jack was just as the man got to his knees. Ben grabbed the man by the wide belt he wore with his left hand and his hair with the other hand and to every man's astonishment jerked the big man over his head holding him with his arms straight. The man was almost eight foot off the ground.

"Do I throw you," Ben screamed.

"No, No," Jack screamed. "I give up.!"

Ben lowered him to the ground. He expected Jack to do something, so he was prepared. He wasn't prepared for what the man did. He stuck out his hand to shake Ben's and said loudly so all could hear.

"I've been 'she bear'" of these here woods for a long time. Now we have a new one." He leaned over toward Ben and asked him his name. "The new 'she bear' is named Ben Watkins." The men rushed in to shake Ben's hand. Ben didn't know at the time, but he was being watched by Jim Bridger and Shakespeare McDovitt who were well known, maybe even better known than any other mountain men.

Ben broke away from the crowd and walked over to the man with the big hat. The man he had talked to earlier was there too. Big hat gave Ben ten dollars and the other man a handful of coins.

That was the easiest ten dollars I ever earned, Ben though and smiled.

"Can yu fite with yur fist?"

"Do what," Ben asked.

The man held his fist up in front of his chest. "Can yu fite with yur damn fist?"

Ben nodded and replied. "Some. Been in a fights before."

The man rubbed his hands together and said. "We mite make sum more money when tha fist fiten starts."

"Maybe," Ben said. "I'll see you around."

Ben slept unusually sound that night. It might have been because for the first time in a while they were a lot of people around or it might have been the fact he was just plain tuckered out. For whatever reason he did not wake up till shouting woke him up. He sat up and scratched his head.

"Glad to see you move. I thought maybe you were dead," the old man chuckled. "Get your cup and have some of this here coffee."

Ben stood up and scratched his head again, rolled his shoulders and picked up his cup and walking over to the old man's camp held it out to be filled.

"Heard you killed that sumbitch Running Fox," he said. "That sumbitch killed or had killed a lot of trappers, some friends of mine. Want to say thanks. A lot of men have tried to kill him but he was always giving them the slip."

Ben took a sip of the strong coffee. "Wasn't much of a deal. I didn't know who he was. He was an Indian fixing to split my friends head open when I killed him."

"No matter. You killed him and that's what's important. Thanks."

Ben nodded. "You're welcome," and smiled and took another sip of the life giving liquid. Nothing was quicker to wake a man up than coffee unless it was a screaming bunch of Indians charging you.

"What's all the hooting and hollering about," over yonder," he asked nodding his head in the direction it was coming from.

"Bare knuckle fighting contest is starting."

"Think I'll wander over and take a look-see," Ben said sipping the last of the coffee and walking back to his camp and putting it up. "Thanks for the coffee," he said to the old trapper as he passed back by heading toward the ruckus.

He watched three fights before deciding these men didn't know a lot about fist fighting. There was more wrestling and holding onto each other than swinging fist. He walked over and paid his dollar. The little man was there.

"Was hoping you would show up."

About that time Ben's name was called. He stripped his buckskin shirt over his head and stepped into the ring. He was looking at a man about his height but probably twenty pounds less than his two hundred.

His little friend sided up to him. "That's Big Bob Tillerson. He's tough but fights a little dirty. If you knock him down watch his hand when he gets up. He'll throw some dirt in your face to blind you for a second. He's won this contest two of the three years we've had had it."

"Thanks," Ben said walking toward the man who was coming toward him as lot of noise begin as the men were talking as money was bet on the fight.

The two men circled to the right and then back to the left sizing each other up. Ben figured this man was in his mid-thirties, but it was hard to tell with the thick black beard that covered his face. He was still sizing him up when a fist hit him in the left jaw. Lights flashed and was he knocked backwards two or three steps almost going down. He shook his head to clear it when he saw the man stepping in to finish it.

Big Bob Tillerson was confident this teenager was finished. He looked over at his friends and winked. That was when Ben hit him on the side of the jaw with a right fist with all his weight behind it. Bob was knocked flat for only the second time in his life. He came up with a roar and as Ben's friend had warned him threw a handful of dirt in Ben's face. Ben saw it coming and shut his eyes preventing the stinging stuff from getting in his eyes.

Bob confident that his opponent could not see charged like a buffalo and straight into another right to the jaw followed by a left to his belly. He went down again. He tried to get up but when he was halfway standing two more blows struck his face. The last one square in the mouth busting his lips and loosening some teeth. He went down again and stayed there.

Ben was declared the winner of the contest because no one was going to fight him. Little did he know that two men were watching that would forever change his life.

That afternoon Ben was making his rounds through the wild camp when he was accosted by Big Bob and two of his friends. Bob had been receiving a lot of ridicule for letting a teenager whip him and he was going to teach this youngster a lesson.

He let loose a right at Ben which Ben ducked and hit Bob in the belly with a right of his on. The man doubled over, and Ben caught him in the face with a knee that smashed his already busted mouth. The two friends jumped in the melee when their friend went down.

Ben caught a fist on his left jaw that only infuriated him, and he became like a cornered she bear with cubs. He caught the man who had hit him with two punches to the face that were so fast it was like one blow. The other jumped on his back with his arm around Ben's throat which was a mistake. Ben, throwing his head back viciously caught the man square on the nose with the back of his head. With a howl of pain, the man loosened his grip on Ben's throat and Ben immediately grabbed the man's arm and threw him over his shoulder and slamming him hard on the ground.

Bob was on his feet now and back into the fight which had drew a large crowd of cheering men. The other man who had earlier hit Ben from his blindside was also on his feet. They circled Ben who was turning on the balls of his feet keeping them in front of him waiting for their rush. In the meantime, the man Ben had thrown over his shoulder was up and coming up behind the unsuspecting youngster.

The two men charged at the same time and the third was wrapping his arms around Ben pinning his arms to his side. Ben roared like a grizzly and twisting his body. The man pinning his arms feet came off the ground and he was parallel to the ground and swinging in a circle catching Bob and his friend with his legs and knocking them to the ground. Among howls and laughter from the other trappers the three were on their feet immediately and started to attack Ben again. It did not happen.

Bob and one of his friends dropped as if a sledgehammer had hit them and the third was lying on the ground having waked into a hard right fist of Ben. Ben was livid at the two trappers who had clubbed Bob and his friend with their Hawken's.

"Calm down my friend," one of the tappers yelled as Ben was coming at them.

"You spoiled my fun damn you," Ben yelled back and kept coming as the two men backed up.

"We just wanted to end the fight before you killed them," the older and smaller of the two said. The other trappers had suddenly got very quiet, watching and listening.

"I was doing okay before you butted in."

The other trapper spoke up. "Yu shornuff wus son and we are sorry we spoiled yur fun but yu wus going to end up killing them thar sorry ass fellers."

Ben stopped and thought for a moment then laughed. "Thanks," he said offering his hand to the two men. "Ben Watkins," he said.

The smaller of the two extended his hand, "Jim Bridger."

Ben was at first shocked at the name then said, "Sorry I yelled at you Mr. Bridger." He looked at the other man. "You must be Shakespeare."

The man nodded his head and took Ben's hand in a firm grip. "That's my name."

"You new out here," Jim asked?

"About as new as a man can get. My friend Jeb called me a greener," Ben chuckled. Jim roared with laughter as well as many of the men gathered around them. That is all but the three men who were sprawled out on the ground.

Someone from the crowd yelled, "Well you may be a greener but if I'm in a fight I want you on my side." More laughs and amends came from the crowd.

Jim put his hand on Ben's shoulder and asked who he was trapping with or was he trapping by himself.

"Was hoping to find someone since Jeb told me it was the smart thing to do."

"I like the way you handle yourself Ben," Jim said. "You killed that bastard Running Fox and saved Jeb from getting his head bashed in. Jeb said you had a lot to learn about trapping but was hell on wheels in a fight though," he said chuckling.

"Reckon I do at that, but I let a man sneak in and steal a bundle of fifty plews from me."

"You didn't catch him?"

"Nope. Big rainstorm came up and washed out his tracks. I know one of his horse's tracks though. Figured I'd mosey round some while I was here and see if I could find that horse. I also had my initials burned in on the inside of each pelt."

Jim nodded. "Never thought of doing that myself. Not a bad idea. If you find that horse you let me know before you do anything foolish, okay?" He turned to Shakespeare. "Let's find something to eat. See you later Ben."

Ben watched them leave and wondered if Jim Bridger was going to ask him to join his party. "Nah, I could not be that lucky" he muttered to himself and walked to where a large group of horses were.

Gary McMillan

Walking among them for several minutes he could not find any sign of the horse's track he was looking for but there was a hell of lot of horses remaining to look at.

Chapter Fifteen

He walked among the horses till it was too late to see and did not find the track he was looking for. Walking back to his campsite he contemplated what it would be like here during the winter and maybe trapping with two of the most famous of the trappers, Jim and Shakespeare. *Only thing I know is what I have heard. The winters are long and cold, the grizzlies are to be left alone, and the Blackfoot are to be avoided at all cost if possible. Then you throw in the packs of wolves, the Utes and the Bloods. I don't think I want to try it by myself. Jeb more or less said that was just asking to be killed.*

Arriving at his camp he found two men there. They stood up when he walked in. Ben quickly found out they were friendly and the three shook hands. One was named James Sandifer and the other George Brooks. James was the older and started the conversation. Ben figured James to be about twenty-five or so and George a couple years younger.

'I'll cut straight to the point about why we are here Ben. We've been here a couple years and we have had others trapping with us. Some went their own way and three were killed. It's just me and George now and we were wondering if maybe you would join up with us. Seen you fight today and if'n you can shoot half as good as you fight, we'd be right proud if you would join up with us."

Ben thought for a few seconds before answering. He was flattered they asked and would consider it if he was not asked by Bridger. He didn't want to burn any bridges so to speak by just saying no. "I'm flattered you asked," he replied. "I have been thinking about trying to find men to trap with. Didn't figure it too smart to try it by myself. Let me think about it and we'll talk some more later. Right now, I'm plumb worn out from what happened today and just want to hit the blankets."

That seemed to satisfy them and said they would see him tomorrow or the next day to talk some more. After they left Ben lay on his blankets looking up at the black sky with its thousands of stars and thinking about the events of the day.

A couple hundred yards away two more men were talking.

"Yu thinking bout asking that yungster to join up with us?"

"Been thinking on it," Bridger answered. "He sure enough can fight which is a good thing. Heard he was a little light on plews but you heard him say he had a bundle stolen. Figured you could sorter take him and teach him the what to do's and not what to do's."

"Me! Its yore idee to take him in."

"You are a lot older and I figure he would listen to you. I'm asking you to try and help him learn what he needs to know to survive out here. "

Buff snorted. "Alrite I'll try dang'nt, but it's agin my better judment."

"Thanks Buff. I think that boy can be of help if we run into trouble. Let's go find him. "

"Won't be hard. He rite over thar kamped by sum uf tha boys," Buff said pointing with his rifle. They headed over there.

Arriving where Ben was, they found him lying on his blanket being questioned by a group of young trappers they stopped and listened.

"Like I said before I didn't know this Running Fox from any other Indian. Only found out who he was when Jeb told me."

"What did Mr. Smith say to you?

"That this Indian was responsible for the killing of a lot of trappers and they were going to be some dang happy trappers when they hear he's dead. I really didn't think that much about it at the time. I was just glad Jeb was okay."

Jim whispered to Buff. "That's what I like about that boy. Any other would be running around like a rooster crowing about what he did and taking in the praise from everyone. Let's go get him." They walked into the ring the youngsters had formed and everyone stepped aside. The two old mountain men had the respect of all.

Jim spoke up. "Ben can we go somewhere and talk"?

Ben took a second to get over his surprise. "Huh sure Mr. Bridger, Shakespeare." They walked to the edge of camp and squatted under a huge pine.

"Ben," Jim began, I would like you to consider trapping with Buff, me, and our friend Jerome Absher. I like the way you handle yourself, not only the way you fight but don't have the big head like a lot of men would after having killed that scoundrel Running Fox."

"I...I would consider it an honor Mr. Bridger but all of you are experienced trappers and I've been trapping three or so months and didn't do a lot of good doing it. I feel like I would be a burden to ya'll.

Jim slapped him on the shoulder and guff-hawed. "Hell Ben, do you think the three of us fell out of our momma's belly knowing how to trap beaver. If the truth was known each of us dang neared starved to death that first year. If the three of us had not teamed up none of us would have been successful or probably not even be alive."

"We learned together Ben. Put what I knew and what Buff and Jerome knew together, and we made a go of it."

"Well if you don't think I will hold you back I would be honored to join you."

"Then it's done. Go get your horses and gear and bring over there to our camp," he said pointing with his Hawken. We'll meet you there."

Ben walked back to camp not noticing anything or anyone. He was as happy as a man could be. *My God*, he thought, *I'm trapping with the most famous mountain men there is. Who would have believed this?*

Back in his camp he was loading his gear on the pack horses and saddling his horse when Jeb came up to him.

"You leaving a little early aren't you?"

"Not leaving Jeb just moving my gear over the Mr. Bridger's camp."

"Boy, did they ask you to join them?"

"Yes sir."

"God be praised Ben. I was worried about you with you being a greener out here and winter only four or so months away. I was not sure you could make it. A lot of men don't but you being with Jim, Buff, and Stumpy you will do good."

"Who is "Stumpy?"

"That's the nickname Jim gave Jerome. He's good at passing out nicknames. Probably have one for you before long. Ole Jerome is about six foot three and skinny as a rail. Naturally Jim fondly calls him Stumpy. Don't let his physical features fool you though. He is one tough hombre in a fight."

"How did Shakespeare become to be called Buff?"

"Shakespeare shot a buffalo a year or so back and thought it was dead till he plunged his butcher knife in that bull's belly. That Bull jumped to its feet and knocked Buff about fifteen feet through the air then fell over dead. Shakespeare was pretty shook up and had some serious bruising. From then on, he was known as Buff," he said chuckling.

"Sounds like this is going to be a lot of fun."

"Don't get to thinking in terms of fun Ben. This is serious business. It's fun here," he said swinging his arm and hand around at the camps, "But there," he said pointing to the dense forest of pines, it is no game. Like I told you back on the trail, there is a lot of ways to die out here and the Indians and grizzlies are only two of them."

"Pay attention to what they tell you Ben. Learn from them and don't ever think things are good and you can relax because those good things can go downhill in an instant. "He shook Ben's hand. "Congratulations. There is a lot men here who would like to be in your moccasins right now and be trapping with those men. I've got me a feeling about you and its one that I will be hearing about for a long time. See you around before this thing is over. Have a good time."

When Jeb left Ben sat on his horse for a moment thinking about what the man had said. After a moment he realized the meaning of what Jeb had said. *You are a fortunate young man to have the best trappers in the mountains ask you to join their party. There's a hundred or more others in these mountains that would like to be in your place so listen, learn and remember the things you are taught and you will do well.*

Three days later the adventure began.

Chapter Sixteen

July 1827

Three days after leaving the rendezvous and traveling southwest the four trappers squatted around a small fire in late afternoon.

"Wus in these here montons fore yeers ago," Buff said. Trapp'd mor bever than ever befor. Don't figger no trapp'rs been thar since. Beaver shuld had plentee time to raze young'uns two three times over. Membur that Ben: don't trap a place out. Always leeve a few ta make babies."

"How come you haven't been back?" Ben questioned.

"Almost lost my hair ta tha damn Blackfoot," Buff answered. "Wus by me own self back then. Cum ta tha rondevouee with over five hundert plews. Swore I wud never cum back by myself. Started trappin with ole Jim thar and he had his own places. He told me to pick the spot this here year and since I ain't by me own self now I tho't what tha hell, let's try her. Shud be thar by noon tomorr'.

Ben lay awake that night thinking about tomorrow when according to Buff they should be in trapping country. He was anxious to learn more about trapping from Buff and more about staying alive and surviving the many dangers. They did talk about the grizzly though. One should avoid them if all possible. If you can't, don't try to run away. The "grizz" can run as fast as a horse for a short distance. If you can get up a tree but make it a big one because the grizzly will actually knock a small one down and you with it. Best to stand your ground, make yourself as big as you can and scream to the top of your lungs. Sometimes he will just go away and sometimes he won't. When he won't is when you are in trouble.

Dawn comes early when you have laid awake for half the night. They were at a little higher altitude and climbing more each day than when they were at the rendezvous and the mornings were becoming downright cold even though it was early July.

Buff had the coffee going and the first whiff of the boiling coffee reached his nose spurred him to hurry out of his blanket and in his coat as well as his cup.

"Morning Buff."

"Morn'n sunnee," Buff replied filling Ben's cup that was in the youngster's hand. Buff's opinion of Ben had changed a little in the last three days. He didn't know whether or not he knew the first thing about trapping as of yet, but he sure was no novice on the trail. He rode sitting tall in the saddle, not slump shouldered like lot of men did. He took care of his horses before he did for himself which spoke well of a man. He took care of his weapons cleaning them about every night and has watched him honing his blade and tomahawk the second night on the trail.

"We going to be in the promise land today Buff," Jim asked as he came to the fire with his cup?

"Yep, bout mid-day," Buff answered filling Jim's cup as well Stumpy's who came up the same time as Jim. "Shud be sett'in our traps late today."

"If'in the trap'n half as good as yu say I'm gonna kiss your ass," Stumpy chuckled. Everyone laughed.

Then Ben impressed all of them. No one had said anything, but all had seen the unshod pony tracks late yesterday. "Ya'll seen the pony tracks yesterday," he asked?'

"Yeah we did Ben," Jim answered. "See them all the time here in the high country so didn't make no fuss about it." Jim had barely noticed them as did Buff and Stumpy.

"I figured as much. Looked to be a couple days old," Ben replied.

"Sunnee, you shor you ain't no greener," Buff asked?'

Ben laughed. "My pa was quite a man back home. People didn't mess with him part because of his temper and part because he was hell on wheels in a fight. If a man or bear or wolf needed tracking people came to him to do it. He spent all his spare time teaching me to track and read sign. We would wrestle and fight with our fist so hard it would scare ma at times. I learned fast and by the time I was fourteen I could handle myself against most grown men. Can't hardly remember a time I didn't have a split lip or black eye," he chuckled "Even though we wrapped our hands in thick cloth so not to do much damage. Came the time pa had his own bruises."

"Wa'l yur pappy did a hell uf a job Ben after whut we seed uf yor'e fitn' those thar men at tha rondovous," Buff said laughing.

About an hour pass mid-day they arrived at a creek that was no more than two feet deep and had an island in the middle. Buff led them to the island that had a big deadfall on it which offered lots of firewood. The dead fall also offered them some protection as well as for the horses.

After setting up camp they laid out their plans for trapping, Ben would trap from the camp to about a quarter mile upstream and Buff would trap from where Ben's last traps were for another quarter mile. Jim and

Stumpy would do the same downstream. This as Jim explained to Ben would leave no one more than a half mile from camp and would be close enough to help each other in case of trouble.

Buff and Ben left camp to set their traps going upstream and Jim and Stumpy went downstream. Both Ben and Buff were astonished as they moved along the bank.

"Don't thank I ever see'd so manee dang bevers in my entire worthless life," Buff said speaking in almost a whisper. "Set yur ferst trap here."

Ben found a sturdy stick and using the back of his tomahawk drove the stick deep in the mud about four foot from the bank. He tied the rawhide strip to the short chain to the trap and tied the other end securely to the stick. After putting the medicine (bait) down they moved a few yards and set another repeating this process moving upstream till all of Ben's traps were out then they begin the process over till all of Buff's traps were out. Both men set out eight traps.

The next morning Ben had six beavers and Buff had seven leaving both men happy with the expectations to come over the next few days. Jim and Jerome had similar results, so the day was spent skinning the beaver and stretching the plews out to dry. They baited their traps that afternoon. There were warm feelings around the small fire that night that comes when things are good, and you are with friends. Four tired but content men went to their blankets that night.

Things were the same for the next five days: bait the traps and skin the beavers. Each man had at least twenty plews except Buff who had twenty-three. At three to four dollars per plew that that was good pay for their work.

The morning of the sixth day broke with clear skies and something else: screams of fifteen or so Blackfoot warriors splashing through the knee-deep stream with one thing on their mind, kill, kill.

Chapter Seventeen

Blackfoot Fight

This would be the morning Jim, Buff, and Stumpy would find out exactly what they had in Ben Watkins.

At the first sound from the Blackfoot each man grabbed their rifles and pistols and lying behind the scattered logs opened fire on the damnable Blackfoot warriors. All being good shots all scored hits. They grabbed their pistols and fired almost at point blank range as the Indians came out of the water and three more went down. After that it was a trapper's nightmare-hand to hand fighting with a Blackfoot warrior.

The attacking Blackfoot as well as the trappers were temporarily startled when they saw Ben jump over the log he was behind standing up all six foot two screaming as loud as the warriors and swinging a butcher knife in his right hand and a tomahawk in the other.

Then, Jim and the others were busy themselves as the warriors swarmed out of the water screaming and banishing their knives and tomahawks.

Stumpy had a warrior leap at him and the warriors tomahawk struck a glancing blow on the side of Stumpy's head. The blow stunned him for a couple seconds but recovered just in time to thwart another blow aimed at his head with his left forearm. He immediately struck with his right hand that held the butcher knife driving the blade to the hilt in the brave's hard belly. He ripped the blade sideways opening up the man's belly. The Blackfoot warrior stood there for a second, leaned slightly forward looking into Stump's eyes then toppled to the ground.

Buff had his own problems as two braves were on him pinning him to the ground. He managed to turn his head as the sharp blade of a tomahawk hit the ground where his head had been an instant earlier. He ripped his right hand free from the warrior and slashed at the man's neck, the blade going in deep. The warrior's head flopped at a weird angle as his head was almost severed. A great amount of blood hit Buff in the face and he was temporally blinded. He knew the other warrior was close and he waited for the killing blow to come to him.

The deadly blow did not come. Stumpy, groggy from the blow to the head threw his butcher knife at the warrior standing above Buff and saw the blade strike the man in the chest just as he was raising the tomahawk to bash his friend's head. He saw this and then nothing. He passed out. Buff, finally getting the blood out of his eyes saw Ben slashing with the tomahawk and knife at everything that moved. He threw the dead warrior off his chest and grabbing his knife rushed to help Jim just as he got to his friend Jim tore his hand holding his knife from the brave's hand that had been gripping it. He drove the knife deep in the man's thigh and from the amount of blood must have cut an artery. The Blackfoot stepped back and started to attack Jim again but when he stepped forward his leg gave way and he stumbled allowing Jim to finish him with another strike with his butcher knife that drove deep through the man's left eye penetrating the brain killing him instantly.

Buff and Jim rushed toward Ben to help him. They quickly saw there was no reason. The only two remaining Blackfoot were already half-way back to the far bank. Jim and Buff looked at Ben and saw three dead warriors at his feet and Ben still screaming like a madman at the retreating two Blackfoot. The two men looked at each other and smiled. They knew they had a real 'she bear' for a partner.

Ben settled down and stared after the retreating warriors who were on the far bank. He saw one kneel down and come up with a bow and quickly notched an arrow and released it.

"LOOK OUT," Ben hollered! The two men turned toward the warriors just as an arrow struck Buff. Buff uttered an oath as he fell to the ground clutching the shaft in his shoulder and protruded six inches out his back. Jim was immediately by his friend's side.

"Thank God," he said and repeated, "Thank God!" Ben was there also and saw what Jim saw. The arrow was in Buff's shoulder, not his chest and low enough it probably did not hit any bones.

"Yu kno'd whut we gotta do Jim, and quick," Buff said through gritted teeth.

Ben looked at Jim. "What is he talking about?"

"Those two will be back with a whole lot of their friends real quick. I figure about mid-morning, noon at the latest."

"What do we need to do?"

"Gather our traps and get the hell away from here. Get a pack horse and gather yours and Buff's traps real fast and get back here. I'm going to check Stumpy," who was sitting up holding his head.

Ben grabbed one of the pack horses, some leather straps and set out up stream to get the traps. Stumpy was coming around and left with Jim and a pack horse to get theirs after reloading their guns including Buff's and propping Buff up against a tree trunk and a big log in front that offered protection as well as a way he could level a rifle on it since his left arm was useless. He also had two pistols. They left trotting upstream. The arrow would have to wait to come out.

Buff was in some serious pain and it seemed forever before Ben returned and shortly thereafter Jim and Stumpy. The pack horses were loaded down with traps and beaver.

"Get the camp stuff packed and let's get out of here," Jim said. It took several minutes to set up camp and less than five this time to pack and get ready to leave.

"Ya'll stay in the stream for three miles or so. Don't step out for any reason and try not to dislodge any rocks in the stream," Jim said. "I'm taking the horses and heading up the creek for a ways then find me a place to get out that is good and rocky and then circle around and head downstream staying a mile or so from the creek and find you in two to three hours."

Walking the horses downstream Ben asked a hurting Buff why Jim headed upstream. "Tha horses will stir up mud and stiks and that will flote down streem ta whare our camp wus. Tha Blackfoot will see it and think we dun went upstreem. May ful them fer a bit but tha will figger it out soon enuf. Jim trying to buy us sum time."

"How's the shoulder?"

"That thar's tha dummest damn question I ever did heer. Hurts like hell."

When they figured they had gone at least three miles they found a rocky bank and stepped out of the stream being careful not to leave any sign and knowing the sun would dry up the water that run off their buckskins.

"Do you think Jim will have trouble finding us."

"Aint worried abut Jim finding us it's tha damn Blackfut finding us ferst tha wurries me."

A hour later they saw Jim with the horses and plews plus the beaver taken that morning that needed skinning. After the handshakes and glad you made it comments they started working on getting the arrow out of buff's shoulder.

"You ever took an arrow out of someone Ben?" Jim asked.

"No, but had one cut out of my arm by Jeb."

"Well if you are going to be out here you might as well learn and now is a good time for your education to start." He gathered some small stick and using his flint and steel had a small fire going in a few minutes. "Take your knife and cut the shaft off as close to the skin on his back as you can." Ben did as he was told holding the bloody point to keep the shaft still as he sawed the shaft into.

After giving Buff a minute to recuperate and get back to breathing normal after the pain of having the shaft cut and getting ready for the worse to come Jim was instructing Ben again. "Place your left hand on Buff's shoulder to steady him and grab the feathered shaft with your right. I'm going to count to three and on three jerk the shaft from his shoulder all the way out without stopping. Understood?"

Ben nodded his understanding and place his left hand on Buff's shoulder and his right on the arrow shaft.

Jim counted out loud, "One... two.. THREE," and watched as Ben sat back on his heels holding the bloody shaft. "Well done boy," he said slapping Ben on the shoulder, "Well done."

Buff had not uttered a sound much to the amazement of Ben. He cheeks puffed out and he let out some air after holding his breath as Ben jerked the shaft out.

"Now comes the worse part Ben. Old Buff knows what's coming so he knows what to expect. Place your knife's blade in the fire and let it lie there for a minute till it is glowing red. You will take it out and place the blade about an inch from the hole and swipe it across the hole keeping it against the flesh."

Jim noticed Ben looked a little pink around the gills.

"If this is not done there's a good chance of infection setting in Ben plus it will stop the flow of blood." Now do it.

Ben reached down and took the blade from the fire, its point glowing red. He hesitated for just a second, holding the blade a hair from the skin of Buff's shoulder.

"Do it boy," Buff shouted and shut his eyes and again held his breath.

Ben laid the blade on the flesh and moved it quickly across the entrance hole. A loud hissing sound came as the blade melted the flesh and sealed the hole even before the stench of burned flesh reached Ben's nostrils. Buff's eye flew open and then closed as he passed out.

"Quickly do the hole in back Ben while the blade is hot, and Buff is out."

Ben repeated the process and had never been so thankful when the whole process was over. He stuck the blade in the ground to remove any residue and then wiped it on the grass to completely clean it.

"Good job Ben. I know it's tough to do that the first time. Hell, it's not easy the second, third or fourth times, but it one of those things out here that has to be done. So now you know. He squatted down by the fire. "We'll rest here for a while to give Buff a little time, but we will have to be moving even though the three of us know that Buff needs more time.

Buff came around about twenty minutes later. He looked down at his shoulder and then at Ben. "Rite damn gud job yu dun thar Ben boy. Now git my soree butt on a horse an let's get tha hell outa heer afor we have sum kumpnee. The man's toughness amazed him. He wondered if he could do this after having an arrow or bullet taken out. This was a lot different than the non-serious wound to his arm. He would learn he could.

Chapter Eighteen

The next few days were uneventful. The three of them run their traps as well as Buff's. The creek they were on was stock full of beaver and all had done well including Buff who was grateful for their help.

On the fifth day after the arrow had been removed Buff was able to run his own traps, skin, scrape, and stretch his own hides.

That night squatting around the small fire drinking coffee the decision was made to move farther up the creek about three or four miles. They had taken a little more than seventy-five plews between them. Leaving a few beavers would insure the creek here would be good again in a couple years.

The sun was not full over the tops of the peaks when they left to gather their traps. Two hours later they were back in camp with their traps and beaver that had been trapped overnight. By the time they were skinned, and the pelts were wrapped up tightly and bundled it was mid-morning. They would be stretched to dry later at their new camp farther upstream.

Moving as quietly as possible through the woods and staying within sight of the creek Ben was mesmerized by the country. They were higher than he had ever been and even though the sun was shining they all had their coats on. Even though it was mid-July the nights would drop below freezing and did not warm up enough to go comfortably without a coat till mid-morning or so.

Ben watched eagles soar overhead with their huge wingspan, searching for something to eat. He watched a couple of elk off in the distance watching them. The air was crystal clear and the majestic peaks, some over nine and ten thousand feet in height, were all still covered from the past winters snow. The contrast between where the green pines stopped growing and the snow-covered peaks was absolutely beautiful. The sight was enough to make a man forget how dangerous and unforgiving this country could suddenly become.

Jim called a halt about midafternoon as the horses needed a rest since they were still climbing higher and higher. While Ben stayed with Buff, Jim and Absher left to look the creek over for beaver. Even though where they stopped was more than a couple hundred yards away both men could hear the creek rushing over the rocks and plunging downhill.

"Don't thank theer's going ta be beaver heer," Buff said. "Creak is runnin to damn fast fer tha beaver ta be able ta damn it up."

Couple minutes later Jim confirmed that thought when he and Absher rode back into camp.

"Water is running too fast for dams to be built by the beaver here," Jim stated.

"Abut three or so miles futher up thar ar sum small lakes if'in I'm membing rite and eech wun has sum small creeks that trikle out slowly fur a ways afore rushing down tha montan side. Shud be plentee beavs thar," Buff stated in his strange way of pronouncing words. Ben loved to hear the old mountain man talk but had to listen closely as he spoke to understand him. Jim and Stumpy had no problem having listened to him a long time.

About an hour before the sun would drop behind the peaks they come upon a small lake. Traveling along the edge it didn't take long to find the first creek leaving the lake and less than fifty yards down the creek they could see a beaver damn. Walking the horses along the bank and past the beaver dam they could see another and when they passed it there was another one.

Jim held up his hand and the party stopped and gathered around where he sat on his horse, hands on the saddle pommel. "You were right Buff. I don't think these here beaver has ever been trapped or if they have it's been a long time. In three hundred yards there are three dams and a lot of beaver. We will go another half mile and make camp before dark sets in and make plans to trap this creek. They passed three more dams before stopping.

Later, chewing on jerky and pemmican and drinking coffee they made their plans. Since Buff was not fully recovered from his wound yet he would trap upstream for about three hundred yards and Ben would trap farther along the creek to the lake. Stumpy would trap for a quarter mile downstream and Jim would go a quarter mile farther down.

"I figure there's enough beaver here to keeps us busy for almost a week," Jim said.

The four of them went to their pack horse and took everything off their backs. They then picketed them with their other horses and each man set to work on getting their traps, medicine, and everything else they would need in the morning when they would set their traps.

"How's the shoulder Buff," Ben asked.

"Almost gud as new. Onlee hurts a mite when I muve it," he said chuckling.

"If you need any help just let me know."

Buff knew he meant it. "I will Ben, I shorley will."

Ben woke up to the heavenly smell of strong coffee. Sitting up he looked around and saw the other three men were squatting by the fire sipping the hot stuff. Buff looked over at Ben.

"Gud afta noon thar yung'un. Glad yu ar alive."

A little embarrassed for sleeping so soundly and late Ben stood up and stuck his two pistols in his wide belt as well as his tomahawk and slide his butcher knife in the sheath in the top of his right moccasin boot. He picked up his Hawken and wiped the moisture from the dew off it and checked its load. He would clean it when he got back from his traps. His pistols were good as they were beside him under his blanket. He walked over to the others.

Jim said. "Started to check to see if you were dead a couple times but then you would snore once again. God knows you can snore," he added chuckling.

"Guess I was plumb wore out from helping this old geezer the last few days."

Yu best damn watch who yu are call'in an old geezer or I must havta teech yu a lessun," Buff said smiling.

After sipping a little more coffee and as the dark sky was turning gray, they all left to set their traps. After what each had seen yesterday afternoon of all the beaver dams each one of them were more than a little excited about the possibilities.

Chapter Nineteen

About midmorning they were all back in camp and plumb excited at the beaver each man saw.

"Don't thank thay everee did see no humen afore," Buff said chuckling.

"They don't seem to pay us no mind at that," Jim added.

"Thought you said you trapped here before," Absher said looking at Buff.

"Did Sunny but it wus sevral yeers ago. Most whut I did see wur only two-maybee three yeers old beves. Musta been at leest five yeers sense I wus heer.

"You said you almost met your end here," Ben said. "Can you tell us about it?"

Buff sat down on his blanket and took a sip of coffee.

"Musta been in '19 or so. I been trappin fer a cuple yeers when I stumbled on ta this heer vallee and it wus chock plum full of bevers. I had abut hundert plews afta abut three weeks. Never saw anuther humen being till one mor'nin I wus back in kamp skinning the bevers I tuk frum my traps that mor'nin. Lukily I had my gear and plews loded on my pac horse as well as my traps. I brote them in cauz I wus muving further downstream.

Tha ferst arrow tuk my hat offin my head. Barley scapped my scalp. I duck't and turned at tha same time. I wus lookin in tha blackest eyes yu ever did see uf a Blackfut warrior not tweny feet away and cuming fast with his tomahawk rased. I had my rifle and jus shot frum the hip since thar wus no time to aim. Ball tuk that Injun squar in tha throat."

"Anuther came at me and I shut him with my pistal. I jumped in tha saddle quicker yu can spit and started ta get tha hell outa thar whun I wus kncked ofin my horse when a brave hit me like a bull bufflo. Hurt like hell when I hit that thar damn rockee grund but I rolled and kame up with mu butcher knif just in time ta block tha blade uf tha Injun."

He paused and took another sip. "Wal I knu I wus in a pickle caus I wus fiten this heer Injun and luking all around at same time lookin fer his friens."

"This heer Blackfut wus no yungun. He wus a full fleged warrior and me and him wuz in a fite ta tha death.

He drew ferst blud when he sliced that butcher knife across my left wrist." He pulled his sleeve back of his buckskin shirt and showed the scar. "It wusn't serious but hurt like tha dickns. Afta that I went on tha attak an stuk him pretee gud in the rite thigh. I musta hit a mane blud vessel cauz he wus lusing a lot of blud. We circled for a cuple minutes wait'in on tha uther ta make a muve. Uf a sudden his leg just plum buckled and he fell to tha ground an I wuz on him like a duck on stink and drove my knife plum to tha hilt in his hart."

I knu I had ta git away quick-like cause his frens mite show up anee time. I wus lusing blud so I rapp'd sum moss frum tha crick an tied a old shirt around it tite-like, leeped on my hoss and got tha hell away."

"So you let the valley because of one attack," Stumpy said?

Buff took another sip of coffee and continued. "Hell, no I didn't leeve cauze uf that. I went abut eight or nine miles down streem and made kamp. Kleened my wrist best I cud and put more moss on it and rapped it again. Wus plum tucker'd out so went ta my blakets and went ta sleep. Nex morn'in I wuz getting my traps ready and my hoss nikered. When I luked I saw two Blackfut with arrors dru bac. I dove ta my left jus as the arrors whizzed by and stuk in tha trunk of a pine. I dru my pistol and cut luse. One went down and tha uther tuk off. I sited my rifle and stroke tha trigg'r and sent anuther ta the hear-afta. I luked around an saw no uther ones so I reloded my guns, walked over ta my hoss and hugged his neck kause his warning saved my reer end."

I squatt'd by my blankts and tho't abut thangs. If'n thos two follo'd me fum tha uthe plac then I figur'd mor cud follow these two. Thar had been no truble, at leest not much, frum tha Blackfut befor but it luked like thangs had changed fer sum reeson. Not wonting ta fite them eveer day I jus decided ta leeve this vallee."

"I remember that about that time sum trappers raped and killed a Blackfoot chief's daughter and things got pretty touchy for a while," Jim said. Stayed that way till the warriors of that tribe finally tracked them down that done it."

"How did they know they were the ones," Ben asked?

Buff answered. "Cauz won uf them wuz stuped enough to have tha girls necklace arund his stuped neck. It tuk them a long time ta die."

"Anyway, things calmed down till a year or so ago when the Blackfoot (the Siksika), the Northern Pilkani (Piegans), Southern Pilkani, and the Kaiwai (Bloods) formed the Blackfoot Confederacy. They banded together to rid the mountains of the trappers who were killing game they needed."

Jim continued his lecture. "Ben, those are the tribes you have to avoid if possible. Right now the

Shoshoni are peaceable and for the most part the Utes but there are a few young Utes that are feeling their oats and decide to try their luck at killing the trappers like the ones that attacked you and Jeb. We have enough problems with the confederacy so don't go killing the friendlies. We'll help you to learn the differences between the tribes."

The traps were set, the beaver from the last camp were skinned and stretched to dry, and now was the time to try and stretch out on one's blankets and rest. The traps would be run and rebaited before dark set in. They would probably have a few beavers this evening but seeing that beaver is more active from sunset till dawn they should have plenty in the morning.

They rested till midafternoon then set out to run their traps. When they returned to camp each one had two or three beaver.

Ben set about skinning his two. Buff had two and Jim and Stumpy each had three. Ben was learning quick that even though living the life of a mountain man was great in that it gave a man a lot of freedom and God only knows the mountains were beautiful, but it was work, a lot of work: bait the traps, run the traps, skin the beaver and stretch the hides to dry and then start over. Then again, if a man wanted to sluff off a day or so he could without a boss screaming at him. *It was all in all a great life, if you could stay alive that is*. He chuckled at the last thought.

When the sun was still behind the mountain tops four excited men headed for their traps. Ben arrived at his first trap and found it held a beaver as did the second. He was surprised to find his next three traps sprung but empty. He saw no tracks other than his own and was mystified.

Back at camp he found the others in a heated debate. Apparently, his traps were not the only ones that were empty.

Gal-dang steeling trappars is whut it wus," a highly upset Buff was saying. "Puree dee steeling." "Ain't but wun thang to do and that's to find'em and kill'um."

Ben was astonished at what he heard. "Kill them," he said, "Why kill them for stealing a few beavers?"

The three other men looked at him like he was crazy.

"You are new out here Ben," Bridger said putting his hand on Ben's shoulder. "There's no law out here except trapper's law and the first of those is you don't steal another man's beaver. If you do you have set yourself apart from all the others and you will be hunted down and if not killed, will go before a court with other trappers in the jury.

"But Buff said we needed to kill them."

"It's not like we are going to shoot them in the back Ben. All the years I have been out here I only know of three or four instances of men running other men's traps. In each case the guilty trapper would defend himself when caught by shooting at the ones chasing him and would be killed because they know if caught, they would mor'n likely hang. Another thing Ben, they would eventually be surprised by a trapper and the trapper would be shot."

Ben nodded. "I understand since you put it that way. Did anyone find any sign of who did it?"

"I waded across the stream and found some tracks," Stumpy said. "Tracks going in the stream, so I headed upstream toward Jim's traps and found where they came out. Seen where he lay the beaver and tracks of two more men who much have come out of the trees. Each one had a pretty heavy load of beaver by the looks of the deep tracks. Headed due north from the creek."

"One of us will have to stay here to watch the camp while the rest of us go after them. Any volunteers?" No one did. "Well then we will have to draw then." Jim picked up some twigs and made sure they were all the same length and then broke one off so it would be shorter than the others. Mixing them up he held them in his hand. "Each one of you pick one and the short one stays here." They did and Stumpy had the short one.

"Yu wun tha prize Stump. See ya afta while," Buff said as he mounted his horse with the others. They crossed the creek and headed up stream to find the tracks Stumpy said he found.

Chapter Twenty

Trapper Justice

Bridger found the tracks leading directly away from the stream. A few yards away another man's tracks joined the first. Bridger found where the second man had waited behind a bunch of aspens. They looked ahead in the direction the tracks were headed and Buff pointed with his long rifle.

"I'll bet my soree hide if'n tha ain't headed fur them thar clump of bolders." Where he pointed was on the side of a mountain at a large jumble of giant boulders that had been thrown from the bowls of the earth no telling how low ago.

Jim nodded his agreement. "I'd be there if I was them. Good protection and a clear field of fire and you can see anyone coming for a long way off. If they are there this is going to take some doing to flush them out."

Jim led the others to some pines that would shield them from anyone in the camp, if that was where there were.

"What if they are not there," Ben said then added, "We will be losing a lot of ground on catching up with them."

"What do you think Buff," Jim asked.

"I thank them no gud fur nutin skunks ar thar."

"My gut tells me the same thing, so we'll proceed based on them being there."

"Your gut tells you!" Ben exclaimed.

"Yes, my gut," Jim said a little agitated at the youngster questioning him and Buff. "You will learn to pay attention to what your guts tells you even though its sorter against what you think. I can't begin to tell you how many times Buff and my hide has been saved the last three or four years by going by what our gut feelings were about a situation. It's not always right but it is right enough times to pay attention to it."

Ben felt the irritation in Jim's voice, so he stayed quite. After all, who was he to argue with two men who were legends in these mountains among the other mountain men? Both were known back east because of the stories by word of mouth about them and Coulter and a couple others.

For the most part the people back east were fascinated by the stories about these men who they felt had to be as savage as the Indians who lived there. These were city people for the most part who had never seen an Indian or a grizzly and most had never even been in a fight with anyone. A few years later stories by writers like Ned Buntline glorified the life of a mountain man telling of the dangers and hardships. Most were not one hundred per cent true, but they sold copies.

"We'll wait till dark and then Injun up on their camp and see if we can surprise them." Jim said.

"Gud idee," Buff said. "Give them time ta skin our beves fur us," he chuckled.

Ben sat with his back against a pine and picked up a long piece of grass put one end between his teeth and chewed on it. *They act like they are sure they are up there as sure as the sun is going to come up tomorrow.* He shook his head and leaned his head back against the trunk and closed his eyes. It wouldn't be dark for three or four hours yet.

Ben must have fallen asleep because the next thing he knew Buff was shaking him by the shoulder. "Wake up yu sleepy head. Time to get our furs back. Tha men ar up thar and thar is three uf them."

"How do you know," Ben asked?

"Wal, while you wur dreeming Jim and me crept up thar and found their kamp."

"Two are asleep and one is on sentry," Jim said. "We are going to get close as we can without chancing to alert the guard. We will make our plan then.

Forty-five minutes later they saw the man watching the area below them expecting if trouble came it would be from the direction of the creek. They did not know that Jim, Buff, and Ben had made a wide circle and were coming down the mountain from above them. When the three of them settled down behind some waist high boulders they saw the guard with his back to them and the two sleeping men.

Jim whispered, "Ben you place your sights on the man on the right and Buff you take the man on the left. I'll take the guard. Don't shoot till we see if they are going to give up."

"Tha ain't gonna do that," Buff chuckled quietly.

Ben hoped they did. He did not like the idea of shooting a man while they were lying in their bedrolls. He didn't have to worry about that as it turned out.

"Hello the camp," Jim shouted. The guard whirled around at the sound of Jim's voice, but he could only see darkness up the mountain. The two men on their blankets sat up and had their rifles pointed up the mountain also.

"Who are you," the guard asked loudly.

"Jim Bridger," Jim said and before he could say another word the men were scrambling one fired blindly in the darkness.

Jim fired his long gun, and the guard was knocked off the boulder he was on. Buff and Ben fired but both missed as their targets were moving fast and due to the darkness, they were shooting at shadows. Bridger hit the guard only because he was sitting on a rock and outlined against the sky. No sound not even the usual night sounds of the animals and the owls on the prowl for their nightly snacks: dead silence.

The three of them had quickly reloaded their guns. "Don't move or make a sound Ben," Jim whispered so quietly Ben could barely understand what he said.

Five minutes passed then fifteen with no sounds from below. Thirty minutes passed and Ben who always was on the attack was getting restless. *This waiting game is for the Indians not me,* he thought to himself. After another fifteen minutes he laid his long gun quietly on the rocks beside him. He took his butcher knife out of its beaded sheath and moved to his right and started slowly and carefully down the mountain working his way around the boulders.

"That ful kid is going ta get his self kilt," Buff whispered to Jim.

Ben moved as silently as a stalking panther stopping every few seconds to listen and study his surroundings as best, he could in the darkness. Twenty minutes had passed, and Ben was thinking the men had left somehow without them hearing them. Suddenly he heard a whispered voice.

"Jasper, you heard or seen anything?"

"No! Now shut up," Jasper whispered back.

Ben was startled. Jasper's voice was to his left and no more than four feet away. He was trying to locate the man in the darkness when the man shifted his body and Ben located him. Ben raised himself off the ground to a crouch and took one step toward the man. He made no sound, but Jasper must have sensed he was there as he whirled around and was so startled to see Ben he shot to quick and the lead ball whistled by Ben's ear.

Ben didn't give the man time to reach for his knife as Ben's blade sunk deep into Jasper's chest piercing the heart. Jasper was dead before he hit the ground.

Hearing noise the other man whispered, "Jasper, what's going on. Are you okay?"

Ben located the man by his voice and answered in not a whispered voice but loudly. "Jasper is dead and if I don't hear that long gun hit the rocks in three seconds you are going to be also." Ben had pulled his pistol out and had it aimed at the shadow he figured was the other man.

The man spun around and raised his long gun and Ben fired. The blast of the pistol was unusually loud in the morning quietness. Flame shot out the barrel and temporally lit up the area in front of Ben. He saw the man knocked backwards by the heavy .54 caliber lead ball. The pistol was not very accurate at more than thirty yards or so but at close range like this it was a devastating force.

Ben stood over the man who was holding his belly where Bens lead hit him just above the wide leather belt. He was alive but hurting something fierce. Ben turned to look up the mountain and hollered, "Jim, you and Buff come on down."

Three minutes later both men were standing beside Ben looking down at the wounded man. All three knew there was no chance of the man surviving such a wound as all his insides were blown to hell.

"Who are you," Jim asked?

"Bill Stevens," the man replied as he tried but failed to sit up.

"Yu know yu are dun fur. Who's tha uther too men so we can mark yur graves," Buff asked.

"Jasper Runnels he muttered in a low struggling voice. God this hurts!" he shouted.

"Jasper and who else," Ben asked the man?

"Didn't know it was your beavers Bridger," he gasped struggling to speak, "J...Jasper and J...J.. James..," he tried to say the last name but he was gone.

Jim looked over at Ben. "That was a fool thing to do boy," he said in a stern voice. Then he slapped Ben on the back and added. "But I'm dang glad you are okay."

They buried the three men and Jim said a few words over them.

"Lord I don't know these men and sure don't know their relationship with You. They done some things here that ain't right but when they come before You, I hope You look at them with compassion. We commend them to you. We were born and lived knowing this day would come. It came a little sooner than they thought so I hope they were ready to meet their Lord and God. Amen"

"Them thar wur nice wurds Jim," Buff said. "Don't kno if'in its gonna ta help those three tho."

Ben said. "They were thieves and maybe even murderers, but every man should have good words spoken over them when they cross the divide whether it helps them to get through those Pearly Gates or not."

Ben looked over at the stack of pelts. "From the looks of all those pelts they must have hit several trappers. What are we going to do with them?"

Jim answered. "We'll take them with us on their pack horses. At the rendezvous word will get around if any lost pelts and we can talk to them. If their story is believable, we will give them how many they think they lost."

"And if no one says anything about furs being stolen?" Ben asked.

Buff chuckled, "Then by Lord we jus got us sum extra plews ta divvy up amongst our own selves."

They loaded up the plews on the two packs animals and had to use one of the men's horses also. Rough count was one hundred seventy-five plews.

With Buff leading they headed back to their camp where Stumpy waited.

As the three men on horseback leading three pack animals crossed back over the creek Stumpy was on the bank waiting for them.

"Was worried when I thought I heard some shooting. What happened?"

"Wal, yu can shor wait till we get sum koffee in our bellies kant yu," Buff said as he was holding on to his saddle horn as his horse struggled out of the water onto the rocky bank.

Five minutes later they were squatted by the small fire sipping their coffee.

"Well?" Stumpy mumbled.

Jim answered. There were three of them Stumpy."

"Three!" Stumpy questioned.

"Yep!" Buff replied. "Three uf them that ar at tha Pearly Gates now hopin' ta get in. Don't rekon that thar is gonna happ'n tho. They had a lot uf plews and I bet sum por ole trappr's wur kilt by them. Jim said sum gud wurds over them tho tryin ta help them."

"What are we gonna do with the plews," Stumpy questioned. "They ain't ours."

"We will take them with us and at the rendezvous if word gets around some trappers were robbed, we will talk to them and get their plews back if we believe their story."

Stumpy nodded. "That makes good sense. I guess if no one steps forward we can divvy them amongst ourselves." He looked at all three men and they nodded.

"We had already discussed that," Ben stated.

"Wal thar is still plentee uf daylite left so lets run our traps," Buff said.

Four days of trapping left each man with twenty to twenty-five more plews before Jim said it was time to move on as he and Buff as usual left a few Beaver to re-populate the stream.

They broke camp the next morning in a slight drizzle. They ran their traps and brought the beaver and their traps back to camp. The clouds were low and heavy with rain. Nowhere could you see the tops of the mountains.

"Don't expect to see any game today boys," Jim commented. "They going to be laid up out of this weather." No sooner had the last word came out of his mouth when the bottom of the clouds opened up and spilled their contents on the land, the men, and every living thing. Each man pulled their buffalo robes a little tighter around themselves for with the rain came a chill in the air.

Water poured off the low wide brimmed hats the men wore keeping most from running down the collars but when it did the cold water sent a shiver up their spines.

"Wal, the gud thang abut all this here rain is we ain't gonna be leeving no tracks fer the dang Blackfut to foll'r," Buff said.

Chapter Twenty-one

The four men followed the stream for eight to ten miles and found themselves at the edge of a huge lake that the stream flowed out of. The rain had quit earlier, and the sun was out. It was mid-afternoon and without a breeze anywhere the lake was like a giant mirror reflecting mountain tops and pines like a huge picture.

"Wud yu luk at that?" Buf said nodding toward the lake. "Ain't nuttin' purtier than that."

"Have to agree with you Buff," Jim said looking out over the lake. He swung his left leg over the back of his horse's neck and sitting there he took out his pipe and makings and begin packing the bowl of the pipe.

Buff stepped down from the saddle. "This here is as gud a spot as anee. We need ta stretch the plews we tuk off the beve we tuk this mornin'. By time we do that it will be time ta make camp fur tha nite. We can find anuther streem in tha mornin' ta trap."

That night the four squatted by the small fire making small talk. Jim and Buff puffed on their pipes. Ben was looking up at the million stars on the moonless night and no clouds to hinder his view. Stumpy was carving something out of a hunk of pine wood.

"You ever married Jim," Ben asked?

Jim pulled deep on the pipe and let the smoke out slowly. Ben didn't think he was going to answer.

"Not by white man's law," he finally answered. "Lived with a Shoshoni woman for two years. Her name was Kaymana which means butterfly in English. Pretty as a picture she was. She was little less than five-foot-tall but wiry and strong as a bear. She was pregnant when the damn Blackfoot came on a raiding party and she got in the way of an arrow that was intended for me. She died in my arms." He was glad it was dark enough that the men could not see the moisture in his eyes as he spoke of her.

"I sorter went berserk and don't know how many Blackfoot I killed with my knife and my hatchet after I emptied my long gun and two pistols, but it was more than a few. Damn near killed my best friend, Little Bear, who came up behind me and put his hand on my shoulder to stop me as the fight was over. It was a great victory for the tribe and the hated Blackfoot were severely beaten. They believed I had a great part in the victory, but I couldn't celebrate with them with Kalama and my child inside her dead."

"That had to be a heartbreaking thing to go through Jim," Stumpy said solemnly.

"I din't kno abut that Jim. Which tribe did yu say she wus frum?"

"There two main bunches of Shoshone. The Eastern and the Western tribes. She was from the Eastern. They mainly lived in the very portable tepee and the whole bunch could be packed and moving within an hour or so. The Western tribes lived in wickiups which was not so portable. I'm telling you this because we were in process of moving when the attack came. A couple hours earlier and it could have been a disaster for the tribe as most of the men would not have been in camp.

A nearby scream startled the four men and the horses immediately begin stomping around, shaking their heads and snorting.

"Panther," Jim said.

"Yeah, and damn close," Stumpy said putting his coffee down and picking up his rifle.

"They don't attack humans do they," Ben asked?

"Not normally," Jim answered as he picked up his long gun also. "Not unless they are hurt in some way and can't hunt their normal food.

A loud snarl from close by answered Jim's statement.

"I'm gonna git to them horses fore they pull them pickets," Buff hollered.

"I'll help," Ben hollered as he jumped up to follow Buff.

Both men got to the horses and grabbed the picket ropes to hold them. They dropped their pistols so they could use both hands to hold the ropes of the frantic horses.

"Whoa! Calm down!" Both men shouted as they were frantically trying to hold the ropes. One of the pack animals broke loose and ran off into the dark. A few minutes later they heard a different scream: the sound of a horse in a lot of pain.

"Dammit to hell!" Buff shouted.

The horses calmed down now that the panther was no longer growling and screaming in a manner no other animal could.

"Going to see if we can find that damn cat," Buff. You and Stumpy there take care of the animals and make sure no more run off. Ben can come with me and get him some experience with the big cats.

"Be karful Jim," Buff replied.

Fifteen minutes later Jim found where the horse had been jumped. Blood and horsehair were scattered all around along with hoof prints showing the horse going in circles.

"Cat jumped from the ledge up there onto the horses back. Stayed on till the horse finally stumbled and fell and then knowing panthers he bit into the jugular and held on till the horse died from loss of blood or strangulation."

Ben, after a few minutes of studying the ground, saw what Jim had saw immediately and nodded his agreement. He silently appreciated the old trapper's ability to read sign so quick.

"Quiet," Jim whispered. "The cat can't be far off. Stay sharp and move with your rifle hammered back. You may not have time to cock and fire if she attacks." They started off with Jim leading following the blood trail with Ben following doing what Jim told him, watching their backs. Both men knew this had to be a huge cat because the horse was being dragged by it.

Jim figured they would find the cat feeding and could get close if they were quiet. The night breeze, what little there was, was in their face so the cat would not get a whiff of them as they approached. Suddenly Jim stopped and held up his hand. Ben stopped and stood motionless. Ben, his eyes searching in the darkness, was nervous as hell and figured Jim could hear his heart beating two hundred beats a minute.

It was deathly quiet; none of the usual night sounds of small animals scurrying about or the hunters like wolves, bears, and such. Jim kneeled down on one knee and Ben followed suite.

"I don't like it Ben," he whispered. I figured that cat would be feeding on our pack animal, but there's the horse and no cat." Ben looked at the dead animal and thought he could actually smell the blood.

"Best be damn careful Ben. The cat is close and may be wanting something besides horsemeat for supper."

Ben gripped the rifle tighter. Sweat broke out on his forehead even though it was cool, almost cold this time of night. He could feel the sweat running down his collar, and he shivered.

They moved to the horse and Jim was looking around crouched trying to find tracks from the light of the moon. He suddenly stood up and looking up at the big pine towering above them.

"LOOK OUT BEN," he shouted. Ben looked up just in time to see an open mouth with huge teeth and huge paws with its razor-sharp claws extended flying thru the air at him. He jerked his rifle up but too late to get a bead on the cat before she slammed into him like a battering ram knocking him backwards onto the ground and losing the grip on his long gun. A little dazed he opened his eyes and looked into the gapping mouth of the big cat who was astride of him.

A rifle cracked and the huge cat screamed and with a bound was gone. Jim came running over to where a dazed Ben lie.

"You hurt bad Ben" he asked?

Ben, sitting up felt of his head and both arms. "Se...seem to be okay," he said and then added, "I think so."

Jim stood up and reloaded his rifle while Ben picked up his and checked it to make sure things were in working order.

"Where did you hit it?" Ben asked while searching the trees and boulders with his eyes.

"Not sure," Jim answered. "Happened so quick I shot from the hip trying to hit him before he chomped down on your head. He's hurt though and unless it was a killing shot, we have a problem on our hands.

"A wounded animal?"

"Yep and a big one. That cat was half again bigger than any I have ever seen. He's hurt and if he ain't dying he gonna be more dangerous than ever."

Ben said. "Why don't we just get our stuff off the dead pack horse and go back to camp and leave him be?"

"Ben," Jim said. "That's the smart thing to do but you have to look at it this way. Most animals in these here mountains, the cats, the bears, the wolves and other hunters don't usually hunt man, but if one is wounded and can't hunt its normal prey then he just might turn man killer. I wouldn't want to know that a trapper died from this wounded cat because I didn't follow up and kill it."

Ben nodded. "I understand. We going to track him now?"

Jim shook his head. "We're not far from camp so we'll go back and then look for tracks in the morning.

Ben was quietly relieved. "Sounds good to me."

Arriving back in camp the two explained what happened. "This is a big cat," Jim said, "Probably the biggest I ever seen or heard about and he is smart. We'll be on his trail come first light. One of us will need to be of guard duty tonight cause he just might decide to come back and pay us another visit. I shot quick and from the hip in order to keep Ben from being mauled so I'm not sure where I hit him. For all I know he could be dead, but we can't afford to lose another pack animal if he isn't. Ben you take the first watch and wake up Stumpy in two hours or so and then Buff and I'll take the last watch."

The night passed quietly as each man took their turns watching the horses. Dawn was slow coming because of heavy clouds that promised more rain at any time. The men saddled their mounts and loaded the bundles of plews on the pack animals. They headed to where Jim and Ben had the encounter with the big cat. Each hoped they would find him dead.

Chapter Twenty-two

When they arrived at the scene all were studying the tracks of the cat.

"Shor nuff a bigg'n Jim," Buff said. He kneeled and placed his hand on one of the tracks. His hand did not cover all of it. "Damn!" he mumbled. "I shor hope like hell he's dead."

"He went off this way," Jim said pointing with his rifle.

"Lookee here," Buff said. "He's missing half uf his rite hind fut," pointing where the tracks of all four paws were plain in the damp ground."

"Probably caught it in a bear trap," Jim said. "No way can he run fast enough to catch a deer and if it was recent probably so sore he can't catch anything."

"All this is pointing to the fact that he is a real danger, right?" Ben stated.

"That's a fact Ben, Jim replied. "A real dangerous animal what with the lead I put in him hurting him and maybe the missing paw also if it was recent. He's gonna be hurting and pissed boys so we had better be on our toes."

They headed out following the tracks and an occasional trace of blood. Each man had their long rifles across their thighs and the hammer cocked. Jim was in front, then Buff and Ben with Stumpy bringing up the rear.

Two hours of nerve-racking tracking brought them no closer to the cat, but they knew he was not hurt bad because he was still moving pretty well. The traces of blood were no longer visible.

They stopped and rested the horses and squatted by their mounts holding the reins and chewing some jerky. They did not need a sudden snarl from the cat stampeding their mounts. Ropes from the pack animals were tied securely to each man's pommel on the saddle to secure them.

"How far behind him do you two figure we are?" Stumpy asked.

Buff answered. "Not so fer that we can relax. He's problee got his eyes on them thar pack hosss's now since he got his self a taste uf hoss meet."

Everyone was quiet for the next few hours. Going was slow because the trail of the big cat was becoming harder and harder to follow. About an hour or so before sunset Jim raised his hand to halt.

"We have about an hour before dark so let's make camp here. There's a stream over there and I could use some coffee. Besides the horses been going for hours. They could use some rest." Nobody argued the point because it wasn't only the horses that needed rest. Tracking a big wounded cat and watching for Indian signs at the same time can wear a man down.

After unloading the pack animals and unsaddling the horses they led them to water and let them drink their fill then picketed them on a patch on good grass. Ben built a small fire surrounded by rocks to keep prying eye seeing it. It was almost dark, so no one worried about what little smoke came from the dead wood they were using.

"Best we sleep close to the horses tonight and every night till we kill this cat," Jim said.

"Wal, with four of us each will only have to watch for little over two hours. Hell, even tha yung whippersnapper Ben there shud be able ta sta awake that long," he cackled slapping his leg. All laughed.

"If he don't that old cat just might sneak up and take a big bite out of his butt," Jim said laughing. Ben, you take the first watch and then Stumpy. Buff you relieve Stumpy then wake me. I'll take the last one."

That said camp was set, the coffee was hot and the men squatted by the small fire sipping coffee and chewing on bacon and biscuits dipped in hot bacon grease which if you didn't have venison or buffalo was cherished by the trappers. After some small talk they began drifting off to their bedrolls one by one till only Ben was awake.

He checked the horse's pickets and walked around the camp staying out of the little light the small fire put out. He was a little nervous because they all knew the cat had not run off. Jim had told a story about a friend of his that was stalked by a cat that he had wounded for several days before the cat attacked his horses and was shot by his friend and another trapper.

His senses were alert, especially his hearing. Every sound was amplified from the creatures of the night like the sound the wings of owls made while flying looking for a meal to the far off cry of a wolf pack to small creatures scurrying through the pine needles. He was attuned to everything going on around him. He carried his long gun in the crook of his left arm with his right forefinger of his right on the trigger and his thumb on the hammer. He was tired and kept circling the camp afraid if he sat down, he would go to sleep.

Ben woke Stumpy up about what he figured 10:30. Stumpy yawned, stretched and scratched himself before he got his skinny frame up.

"All quite Stumpy," he said quietly. He lay down on the grass and pulled his wool blanket up to his chin and was asleep in a couple minutes.

Stumpy stretched again, picked up his tin cup and poured himself what was left in the pot sitting on a rock by the small fire which Ben had kept burning as would he. He had the cup to his lips while looking at the horses and he saw their heads come up and ears start twitching. He bent down to set his cup on the rock when all hell broke loose. The cat came out of the darkness and slammed into Stumpy before he had a chance to move never less bring his rifle to up.

A huge paw struck him on his right shoulder and knocked him thru the air a good ten feet where he hit hard and rolled a couple times. The cat was on him immediately and he could feel the cat's hot breath on the back of his neck. Suddenly a rifle shot split the night air and the cat was gone.

Ben had reacted quickly and fired his rifle in the air hoping it would scare the cat away which it did. He had been afraid to shoot at the cat because Stumpy and the cat was outside the fire light and he was afraid of hitting Stumpy.

The three men rushed to Stump's side to see if he was okay. Jim rolled him over and the injured man looked at him. " Wh..What h..happened?"

"Don't you remember?

Stumpy raised himself to a sitting position and started to rub his head with his right hand but could only lift it part way because of the pain. In his shoulder. "Damnation" he hollered.

Jim gently laid him back on the ground. Buff brought a stick from the fire that was burning on one end. Jim, who had some experience doctoring wounds over the years felt around on Stumps shoulder.

"I don't think anything is broken Stumpy, but I think your shoulder is out of place. You ain't gonna like this but it has to be done for it to heal proper. He lay Stump flat on his back and had Ben hold his head after placing Stumps right arm fully extended out beside him he placed his foot under Stump's arm pit. He placed both his hands around the man's wrist. I'm going to count to three Stumpy and pull your arm to get your shoulder back in place.

Stumpy nodded and set his jaw.

"One," Jim said and pulled the man's arm toward him. There was a small popping sound, and it was done.

"I thought you said on three." Stumpy hollered. Jim laughed.

"Feels a little better don't it." Jim asked.

Stumpy sitting up now moved his shoulder around. "Yeah, I guess it do," he said smiling and grimacing at the same time.

"Now tal us whut happn'd," Buff said.

"Well, Ben woke me up and I poured what was left of the coffee in my cup and was fixing to take a sip when I saw the horses heads come up and their ears twitching. I sat the cup back down and the next thing I knew I was flying thru the air. And then the cat was on top of my back."

"Good thing that big paw of his hit you on the shoulder because any higher it would have broken your sorry neck." Jim stated.

"You tu," Buff said looking at Ben and Stumpy," Do yu have anee idee whut just happened?"

The two youngsters looked at each other and back at Buff and saying nothing. To them it was obvious what happened.

"Wal let me tell yu two sumptin. That thar cat did sumptin I ain't seed befo. He kame into our kamp and attaked Stump thar who wus rite by tha damn fire. Cats ar afrid uf fire and us humans but this one ain't." He looked at Bridger. "Whuts yur fix on this cat."

"I heard this happening one other time from some trappers. Cat tracked them and killed one of them before they finally killed it. They called it the 'Devil Cat'. The cat followed them for a week keeping them and the horses awake at night staying in the shadows and screaming every once in a while, just to let them know he was around."

Jim looked at the horses who were calm now. "We were hunting it but now the table has turned, and it is hunting us. We have got to try and find him before he attacks again and possibly have disastrous results for us. So let's load up the pack animals and saddle our broncs at first light and find the damn thing."

"I don't think he will come back tonight," he added, "But we can't take any chances. Stump, me and you will watch the camp for three hours and then Ben and Buff for about three hours. By then it will close to sunup and we can fix a little breakfast, have some coffee and be ready to leave at first light to find the dang cat."

The night passed without the cat coming back. The four men squatted by the fire sipping coffee eating bacon and dry biscuits that were made tasty by soaking them in the bacon grease. The pack animals had been packed with the beaver plews and the horses saddled.

"I was thinking about this situation while Stumpy and me were on watch last night," Jim said downing the last of his coffee. "This here cat is following so I think two of us should find a place to hide while other two go ahead with the pack animals. Maybe we can kill him if he continues to follow us. What do you think?"

"I know I don't have the experience all of you have but I was thinking along the same line only I was thinking about sitting in a tree around our camp and shooting it when it came back," Ben said.

Buff said. "Tha thars a good idee Ben but tha wud have yu mabee shooting in tha dark. I like Jim's idee whar it wud be shooting in daylite."

"Me too," Stumpy said. "I would like to be one of them that stayed behind since that damn cat nearly killed me. I owe him."

"Since it's my idea so I will stay behind and if it's okay with Buff and Ben, Stumpy you can stay with me." Buff and Ben nodded their heads. "Then we will find a place along the trail and set up our trap for him." They mounted and headed out.

About a mile down the trail they found a good spot. About seventy feet above the trail was a hole in the side of the cliff where a huge boulder had come loose a long time ago and crashed down the mountain knocking down a couple pines that was in its path. The small hole in the cliff would give them good cover and with the trees down a good field of fire. Jim thought it was perfect.

The two men took a canteen with them and scrambled up the side of the mountain to the hole and Ben and Buff continued down the trail with their friends horses the pack animals.

Jim and Stumpy made themselves comfortable and laid their long guns in front of them as they lay on their bellies.

"How long do you think," Stumpy whispered?

"Hard to say," Jim whispered back. "Could be a few minutes or late today or he might not come at all."

The day passed and the only thing they had seen were four elk and a couple of coyotes. At midafternoon Jim nudged Stumpy and whispered.

"I don't think he is coming, and we need some meat and there's a pretty good size buck walking along the trail. I'm going to shoot him, and we will dress him out and head up the trail to find Buff and Ben.

Jim took a deep breath and let it out slowly as he sighted in on the buck. He slowly stroked the trigger, and the round fifty caliber ball was on its way to the target. The buck jumped straight up when the ball hit him just behind the left foreleg. He stumbled a few steps and was down. Stumpy started to get up but Jim grabbed his arm.

"Wait a few minutes to see if something else comes along," Jim said while reloading his Hawken rifle. They waited twenty minutes and then headed down the side of the mountain to where the buck lay. They begin dressing out the buck when they heard the growl. Both men looked up and saw the cat in midair coming right at them.

Chapter Twenty-three

The big cat hit Jim in the shoulders with his front paws knocking him ass over heels backwards. The cat was straddle of his chest fixing to bite into the soft flesh of his neck when a yell from Stumpy caused him to turn his head toward him and forgetting Buff who was flat on his back leaped toward Stumpy.

Jim pulled his short gun from the leather belt around his waist and pulled the trigger with a hastily aimed shot. The cat bit into Stumpy's calf just as the bullet creased his left hip. Releasing Stumpy's calf he let out an unearthly scream and bounded off, disappearing in the thick pines.

Jim recovered his Hawken, checked the load, and crawled over to Stumpy who was holding his severely bitten calf. Jim's friend was evidently in shock and the pain had not hit him yet. Jim knew it was only a moment away though and rummaged thru his possible's bag for the pint of whiskey he carried for cold nights or for emergencies such as this. Nothing better than firewater to cleanse a wound. When he turned to Stumpy, he knew the shock had worn off as Stump was sitting cross legged and holding his calf with both hands, rocking back and forth groaning.

"Take a few swigs of this here Stump. Help with the pain sum." Stump downed almost a third of the whiskey before Jim could take it away. "Save sum for your leg Stump".

Stumpy lay back on the grass as Jim looked at his calf. The cat had bitten thru his knee-high moccasins and his leather pants. Jim untied the strings and rolled down the moccasins to reveal two deep puncture wounds on the inside of his calf in the muscle and more shallow ones on the outside of the calf. Upon closer examination Jim was relieved to find that the leg bone was not broken.

Without saying a word, he poured some whiskey on the wound resulting some vile words coming forth from Stump's lips. Jim smiled at the outburst but quickly wiped it away. He knew with Stump hurt and with no horses he knew they were in more than a little trouble.

Less than a mile away Buff and Ben had stopped and was waiting on them. They had been here for longer than Buff liked. He figured that damn cat if he was following them should have showed up a couple hours ago. Then, they heard the shot. They could tell by the sound it was a pistol not a long gun.

"Sumthangs wrong Ben. Get tha pack horses. We're headed back down tha trail."

Jim rigged a travois which he placed Stumpy sitting on a buffalo coat which was wrapped around each pole. He gave his pistol to Stumpy and along with Stumps own which gave him two which to use if the damn cat came back. After making sure his friend was comfortable as possible, he placed one end of each poles on each shoulder and tied the ends with a short piece of rope. Holding the rope with his left hand to keep the rope off his neck he carried the Hawken in his right.

Jim was sweating profusely pulling the travois with Stumpy lying on it. *First time I'm glad Stump is skinny as a rail. Don't know if I could pull him if he weighed any more than he does,* Jim thought to himself.

"Keep your eyes open Stump. Dang cat could come at us again any time."

He had stopped to rest for a minute when he heard the sound of horses coming down the trail and not far away. "If its Injuns we are in trouble," he whispered to Stumpy. He pulled the travois around and behind a rock to give some protection for the both of them. Stumpy had both pistols cocked and Buff had his Hawken and Stumps Lancaster rifle both cocked and ready. Both knew with Stump hurt they were in trouble otherwise they could just have moved quickly and quietly into the forest.

They had their weapons trained on the bend of the trail about thirty yards in front of them.

"Let them come around the bend. I'll take the first man and you the second," Buff whispered. Stumpy nodded his head, his pain forgotten for now and was replaced by fear.

"Well I be dammed," Jim exclaimed as the head of the first horse showed as he came into view around the bend. He knew the horse and who was riding it and stepped out in the trail just as the man showed himself. Jim stepping out like that caused the man to jerk on his reins and get ready for trouble before he recognized his old friend.

"Buff, are we glad to see you."

Buff looked at Jim and then at Stumpy smiling. "Whut happe'nd? We heerd tha shot and cud tell it wus a short gun not a rifle so we kame back."

"Set a spell and I'll tell you," Jim replied. "Look at ole Stumps leg first though."

Buff who had seen all kinds of wounds and bites looked at Stump's leg. "I've see'd wurse Stumpy. Yu ar going ta have a sore leg for a while but nuttin appears broken. We jus have ta watch fur infecksion setting in." He turned to Ben, "Ben get sum moss from tha creek over there."

"Moss," Ben questioned. "Why moss?"

"Indians and mountain men been using moss for years to put on wounds." Jim replied. "Don't know exactly why moss works but it does for sure. Helps stem the flow of blood and protects wounds from becoming infected."

"Oh," Ben said and started for the creek.

"Wat a minute youngun," Buff said. "With that thar cat around kno wun needs ta go anee whar by their lonsome, not even ta pee." He went with Ben. This decision proved to be a great one.

At the creek Ben bent over to get the moss when Buff hollered, "GET DOWN BEN and fired his Hawken. The rifle was just above Bens head and the sound almost deafened him. Looking up Ben saw the cat across the creek he saw the cat lying biting at his side then the cat jumped up and in two bounds was in midair coming right at Ben with a vicious snarl and mouth open showing the huge top fangs. Ben froze at the site but then Buff's short gun exploded. The lead ball hit the cat square in the chest, and he dropped dead in the water.

"Yu ev'r eat panter meat Ben," Buff asked calm as could be.

"D..do w..hat." an obviously still shaken Ben stuttered out.

Buff trying to show this young'un he was calm as if he was walking down a street in a city. "I asked if yu have ev'r eat panter meet," using the term some called the mountain lion.

"Can't say I have."

"Then ole pard yuar in fur a treet. Panter meat is better'd than vensun meat."

Ben just sorter had this disbelieving look but followed Buff who had out his butcher knife. He poked the cat with the tip of his blade to make sure he was dead.

"Grab a leg Sunee and lets drag this heer cat ta tha bank and skin him."

Jim was coming in a hurry and stood on the bank looking across the creek at his friends and the dead panther. He bowed his head. "Thank You Lord, Thank You."

Laying the cat on the bank they all stared at it.

"How much you figure he weighs Buff?' Jim asked.

"Wal the biggest I ever did see'd waghed in at abut hundert fifty or sixty pounds. Figure this cat is half again that heavy.

Jim nodded. "I figured about two-fifty at least. No matter, it's the biggest dang cat I ever saw."

That night, Ben was introduced to panther meat and was surprised it tasted as good as it did but being so dang hungry might have something to do with it.

Chapter Twenty-four

Blizzard

The next morning the men woke up to what appeared to be a fairly clear sky as a few stars could still be seen here and there. There was definite chill in the air from the rain that fell yesterday. Ben finally got up and stirred the coals and got a small fire going. He filled the coffee pot with water from the creek and placed it on the fire.

"Been lying here wondering who was going to get up and make coffee," Jim chuckled.

"Me tu," Buff said. "Dang ole bones ake when tha mornings ar kold. Glad yu started tha fire Ben."

When daylight came, they knew it was going to be a great day. Clear sky, no wind just a slight breeze and the warming sun rays taking the chill away.

Ben stood away from the others holding his tin cup of coffee and looking out over the prettiest valley he ever did see. He looked at the tall beautiful pines and the white barked aspens that grew on the banks of the stream that flowed thru it. Two eagles soared high above the valley. He sniffed of the fresh clean mountain air and knew for sure this is where he wanted to be: always and forever. If God ever came to earth to live, this would be where it would be. The thoughts were kicked out of his head when Jim hollered at him.

"You gonna stand there gawking at the scenery boy are you gonna get them traps and get to work. The three men laughed because not a one of them had not stood and looked at God's handiwork many times and thought the same thoughts they figured Ben had been thinking.

Buff and Ben went up stream to set their traps and Jim and Absher went downstream. Each carried eight traps with him. Every hundred yards or so were beaver dams and more beaver sign than any of them had seen before. They knew they had hit a gold mine for prime beaver. Fall was coming on and the beaver's fur would become thicker before the cold and snow set in.

Three hours later they squatted by the small fire talking.

"We'll work this area for a week then move on farther down the stream," Jim said. "It's going to start getting cold in a couple three weeks and the snow will begin falling. We'll get as many plews as we can before then but each of us needs to be looking for a place to go hole up when the snow starts." He looked at Ben. "I don't think you have ever been in a blizzard before have you?"

Ben laughed. "I guess not. Seen it snow a few times though." The other three men laughed.

"Wal sunee let this ole hoss tal yu sumthang. Yu will see sno deeper than a man sitten on top uf his hoss. Yu will see sno fallen so fas and thik yu can't see ten feet. Then thar ar times when tha sno is fallen thik and tha wind is blowin fortee miles per hour and tempature is twentee below. That thar is when yu ar damn glad yu have nice cozee cave to sta in. Mor'n a few trappars didn't and were found in tha spring froz stiffern a bord."

"On of top of that Ben, the game is scarce so if a man don't plan ahead he can starve to death." Jim added.

"The good news is that the Blackfoot and Utes stay close to their warm beds and wives," Stumpy chuckled.

"That's true Stump. I sometimes wish I had a warm bed with a woman in it," Jim said laughing, "instead of three men who hasn't bathed in a month in a damp old cave."

"Ar yu sayin I stink? Buff asked

"No," Stump said. "But have you bathed since we all did at the rendezvous two months ago?"

"Hell no. I bath regularlee tho bout ev"r three munts or so."

Jim cut in and said laughing. "I think it is safe to say all of us could do some bathing and washing of clothes."

They headed to the stream and Jim and Buff stripped off their buckskins and eased slowly into the ice-cold stream while Stump and Ben watched the camp. Then they reversed the order. Jim stated earlier it would be embarrassing if some Blackfeet showed up and us naked and defenseless. They all had got a chuckle out of that statement. Jim checked Buff's leg. It looked okay, just sore.

That afternoon when the men returned from running and re-setting their traps there was much laughter and joking. Each man had either seven or eight beaver to skin. This was an awesome haul for any trapper. Three to four dollars per pelt and each. Each man made about thirty or so dollars for a day's work which was huge pay for them. The average day would be two to three pelts and some days none. A good income would be six hundred dollars for a year's work and most of that would be spent on supplies and whiskey at the rendezvous. They were a happy lot.

Things were pretty much the same for the next three days: get up and run the taps, rebait them and skin and stretch the plews for the rest of the day. Hard work and in between mend clothes and take care of their weapons. There was always one man watching the horses and his plews were taken care of by the others. They had turned into a pretty dang good team.

The morning of the fourth day found heavy grey clouds and a slight north wind that had a chill to it. They had decided to move camp last night and Ben and Stumpy were packing the plews on the pack horses.

"I don't like this, Buff" Jim said softly.

"Don't lik whut?

Jim looked up the sky. "What do you think of those clouds?"

Buff looked up and noticed them for what they were. "YU thanking whut I am?"

"I think we had better hole up and get us a deer or two. Maybe a buffalo if we can."

"Mus be getting old," Buff said. "Nev'r even notce'd them cluds in tha sky."

"My gut tells me this may be an early humdinger of a storm. Clouds look heavy, lots of moisture in the air and the wind is out of the north." He turned and hollered for Ben and Stumpy to come over.

"Buff and me have been talking and we think we are in for an early snowstorm. I'm going to see if I can find a deer or two before it sets in. Ya'll need to find a cave or someplace we can hole up and if it comes, we can ride it out. Follow Buff up the stream and keep your eyes open for a good place. Hopefully we are wrong but both of us have seen these early storms before and they can be killers if you are not prepared. Any questions?"

Stumpy said. "Ben mentioned to me a minute ago while packing the plews about the clouds and they looked like they held snow." Jim and Buff looked each other than at Ben at the same time and both thought the same thing. *This youngster may be knowing beyond his years.*

Jim mounted his horse rode away heading down hill thinking there would be more game at a little lower elevation. The others finished gathering up equipment and utensils and headed up stream with Buff in the lead.

Two hours later they stopped and put their coats on. The temperature had dropped several degrees and was starting to mist a little. An hour later Buff pointed up a fairly steep incline. Forty or so feet up the slope a cave could be seen but they could not tell how deep it was.

It had started to sleet now, and the temperature had fell probably forty degrees since they broke camp and the wind was blowing strong out of the north.

"Hol my hoss Ben. I'm goanna tak-a- luk see at that thar kav." He climbed to the cave and went in. He was hoping there was no varmits in there like a bear or a big cat. There wasn't and he was surprised by the depth and pleased to find that it turned right about twenty feet from the opening which would help keep the wind from blowing directly in on them. He walked to the opening and motioned for them to bring the animals up and they would get ready to ride this thing out if it did develop into a storm. A few minutes later Ben and stumpy arrived with their horses and Buff's along with the pack animals.

"I tal yu boys sumthang. If'n we had luked a yeer we kud not hav found a bettr' plac than this. We kan leeve the hosses' heer at klos ta tha openin uf tha kave. Tha'l sta dry and kozy whil we sta kozy aroun tha thar bend. Let's unlod thos pak animuls an set up kamp."

They heard a shout from below. Ben looked out and Jim and waved at him. The wind was blowing hard now, and he could barely hear what Jim was saying but he did understand the arm waving for him to come down. He made his way down the slope and found Jim had a deer laid across his saddle which he hadn't noticed. He carried Jim's rifle while Jim led the horse up the slope which was beginning to get even slicker with the snow starting to stick to the rocks and the horse wasn't liking it very much.

They went into the cave and Jim looked around with a surprised look on his face. "This place may be cozier than one of them teepees the Indians live in." He walked around the bend where there was a fire going and where all the packs were. "This is perfect for the situation. We need to get down below and a couple of us pull grass along the creek for the horses and the other two get firewood and plenty of it. Ben, you and Stumpy get the firewood and we get the grass." Both of the young'uns started toward the opening when Jim shouted out to them.

"Take your pistols. Won't be no Indians in this weather but could be a cat or bear looking for a place to hole up." They came back and picked up their two pistols each, checked the loads and put them in their wide leather belts and headed down the hill with their hatchets to get wood. Three hours later and several trip up and down the slope with wood and grass four men lay stretched out by the fire exhausted.

Dusk found the weather had turned nasty. The temperature was in the teens and the wind was blowing hard and then gusting harder. The opening of the cave faced more toward the south east than south and most of the wind driven snow was staying away from the horses who seemed fairly content resting and munching on the green sweet grass from the creek bank. There wouldn't be any green grass to be found anywhere tomorrow unless one dug for it.

Jim and Buff had dressed the deer and made a little stew with chunks of venison in it. It was a tasty meal but as hungry as they were anything would be good. They made coffee and talked for a while and then went to their blankets with their buffalo robes on. The howling of the wind whistling down the canyon helped put them to sleep.

If anything, the wind was blowing harder when they awoke the next morning. Ben was the first up and stirring the coals with a stick to get them to flame up then put more wood on and soon had a nice fire going. He walked around the bend and checked on the horses then looked outside. He could not believe what he saw at least what he could see through the heavy snow that was sweeping by the mouth of the cave driven by the wind.

From what he could see the rocky slope they had climbed yesterday to get to the cave was probably two foot under the snow. Some places to his right was very little snow because of the wind but looking to the left which was a little more out of the wind it was two or more foot deep.

Jim walked up beside him. "Had me a feeling yesterday this was going to be a humdinger of a storm and by the looks of things it's going to get a lot worse."

Ben nodded. "Dang good thing for your gut telling you this. I sure wouldn't wanted to have spent the night out there."

"A lot of good men have died in storms like this that could not find a place to hole up. Buff and me found old Henry Langtry and his partner Bill Gleeson just this last spring. The snow was still on the ground, but the weather was mild and the snow was melting. They were huddled together froze stiff even with their buffalo coats on. We had to wait a couple days for the warm weather to unfreeze them so we could lay them out straight and bury them."

Buff and Stumpy came up beside them. "Shor nuff snowed didn't it," Buff mumbled looking at the blowing stuff. "Temp gotta be in tha teens."

"How much grass do you figure we have for the horses, Buff?" Jim asked.

Buff walked back around the bend to take a look and came back. "Bout three days' worth, mabee fore ifn' we stretch it sum."

"I don't know about you boys, but I think we need to consider holing up here till spring," Jim suggested.

"Storm this eerly I wud say we're in fer a bad fall and wenner. If'n we kan find meet ta eat and grass fer tha hosses, I'll go along with that thar idee," Buff answered.

Ben and Stumpy looked at each other and then nodded their agreement.

The next twenty-four hours were the same as the last forty-eight: snow and more snow and the wind, lots of wind. The men got a lot of rest between fixing meals, raking out the horse manure, and cleaning the weapons and sharpening their butcher knives and hatchets. Mostly though they just talked and most of the talk came from Jim and Buff. Talk of things they had seen and experienced the last two or three years and the two younger ones were soaking it up like a sponge, Ben more than Stumpy.

Stories of fights with the Indians, mostly the Blackfoot. The youngsters, mainly Ben seeing how Stumpy had been up the creek and round the bend with them, learned that the Shoshoni and the Nez Pearce were two tribes who were generally friendly to the trappers. But Jim had warned us before that Indians were notional people and moods could change quickly.

They told the story of a trapper named Larry Bonner who along with his buddies were attacked by Utes. Larry was injured pretty badly and two days later they found a Shoshoni camp. They were friendly as could be and their medicine man did his hocus pocus stuff over Larry and one of the women put all kinds of stuff on his wound. Well Larry was running a high fever and they, his fellow trappers, figured they would be burying him pretty quick.

Well, old Larry fooled them all. His fever broke and in another three or four days he was walking around the camp.

"Don't know exactly what happened but those friendly Shoshoni turned on them. Larry could not move fast enough and was full of arrows faster than you can spit. Two others of the group were killed, and one seriously wounded before they got away from the camp. For some reason the Shoshoni warriors did not follow them. The only thing they could figure was that their "mad" was short lived and was satisfied with three dead trappers."

"I'm telling you this so you will never totally trust the Indian. We are in what has been their land for a long time. I can understand why they feel the way they do. We are killing game they need for their very livelihood: to feed themselves, for shelter and for the clothes they wear, even weapons they use. You can't hate them for attacking and killing trappers. You have to understand we are the ones intruding on what they believe is their land."

"Funny you say this because when I was trapping with Jeb Smith early this year for a month or so he told me pretty much the same thing."

"A lot uf trappr's feel this heer way Ben, but thar ar a lot uf them who jus as soon kill them as luk at them."

"Buff's right," Jim said. "There are Indians that are friendly and like the white man and others like the Blackfoot who hate us with ever fiber in their body. There are trappers that are the same way and ones that go out of their way to kill an Indian which causes trouble for all of us."

"Ben," Buff said "Do yu miss anee thang frum whare yur frum back East?"

Ben thought for a minute. "I miss my family more than anything. I wish they could see these mountains." He meant those words too. He missed them but not the hustle and bustle of the city even though they lived outside of town. He had seen the greed, the lust for money and power. People were crammed together like rats in a cage. All were wanting more than their neighbors. It was a rat race, and he was glad his family only had limited contact with city folk. He continued. "I've learned out here a man can be himself and is free to do what he wants when he wants."

"Free. I never knew the meaning of that word till I came to these mountains. People in the cities are not really happy with their lives since most just struggle to survive another day. In these mountains almost everyone I have met is friendly and happy just to be here. I know it takes a lot of work to be successful in these mountains, but it is possible I have learned." He chuckled, "One just has to watch out for Indians trying to scalp him, critters trying to eat him, weather trying to freeze him to death and a half dozen other thing that can kill him. What is there not to love about that," he asked laughing? The other three trapper laughed, and Buff slapped him on the shoulder.

"I cudn't have sade that better my own self," Buff said still smiling.

'Jim, how many fights with the Indians have you and Buff had," Stumpy asked? "I know it more than a few because I was with you last year and we had two pretty close calls and a couple this year."

Jim was quite for a moment and stood up and refilled his coffee cup with the strong coffee and then squatted back down.

"I'm not sure," he finally said. He looked at Buff who was counting on his fingers. "What do you think Buff, maybe fifteen or so?"

"Sounds rite if'n yu don't kount tha fites we have had with jus wun Injun at a time."

"I would say twelve to fifteen encounters with groups of five or ten and one with thirty or more."

" How in the world did you two fight off thirty or so," Ben asked.

"Weren't jus me an Jim," Buff said. "A grup uf us wur goin ta tha rondevoss two summers ago."

Jim cut in and said. "That's right. We had all our plews on pack horses, some of us had two or three, so we made quite a little caravan that was too tempting for the Blackfoot to pass up. We were riding through a high meadow where the grass was three or four feet high. Those Blackfoot had a trap set for us and we blundered right into it like some damn tenderfeet trappers."

Buff howled with laughter causing everyone to look at him. He settles down long enough to say, "Tha wun thang them Blackfut didn't kount on wus Jim. He fired his long gun at tha closet wun as we all did."

Jim said. "I think they thought we would dismount and fight them, but I kicked my horse and ran right at them and the others followed his lead. Well, like I said there were ten of us and each had more than one pack horse and they were on foot. It was a stampede thru the grass and a lot of them were bowled over by the horses, a few were shot, and the rest scattered like a covey of quail.

We raced the horses for about a hundred yards and pulled up and turned around. What we saw was a bunch of Blackfoot walking around helping their friends up: some holding their heads, some limping and some with probably broke arms. We had one man with an arrow in his thigh. Later we were recounting the fight, if you could call it a fight, and we probably shot four or five, so they did not come out on the good end of that encounter."

It was midafternoon when they all realized something was different. It only took a few seconds for them to realize the wind had stopped. They walked to the opening and looked out at a winter wonderland. It was still snowing heavy but with no wind it was falling straight down and stacking up on the rocks they had climbed on to get where they were. It had been fairly windswept till now and now the snow was really piling up to maybe a foot deep.

"Rekon we outa go down thar and git sum grass and wood whilest we can," Buff mentioned.

"Good idea Buff," Jim said. "Well do the same as before. Buff and me will get the grass and you two get the wood. Keep an eye on the clouds. They are still heavy, and the wind could come again real quick like and you don't want to be far from here. We'll tie a rope up here and throw it down to use to haul wood up here so gather what you can and put it down where the rope is. Buff and I will get enough grass for a few days and then we will haul the wood up as you bring it in.

They worked for two hours before Buff and Jim had what they thought was enough grass and with Buff at the bottom tying bundles together and Jim hauling them up. A breeze had come up out of the north and the clouds seemed to become heavier.

Stumpy came up with another load of wood and Buff asked, "Do you know where Ben is?

"Downstream, I guess. I've been working upstream. Why?"

"Damn storm is coming in again and I bet it's going to be a doozy and Ben could get caught in it. Let's get this wood up there and then go get him.

Fifteen minutes later they had the wood stored away and started to the cave opening when of a sudden the wind hit with the horrendous force. Looking out they could not see the end of the rope at the bottom of the slope because of the heavy blowing snow.

"Jesus!" Stumpy exclaimed.

"Ben is in serious trouble ya'll. Bring your pistols up here with powder. Don't need no balls just powder and paper. I just want to fire shots to see if we can lead Ben here.

Ben cussed at himself for not doing what Jim said and watch the clouds and wind. He figured he was no more than a hundred or so yards from the cave, but he could not see ten feet in front of himself and its suddenly cold...damn cold that was cutting to the bone. He struggled not only against the wind but struggled to force his legs just to move. He just thought he had been cold before.

Jim fired one of the pistols and then a second before handing them back to Stumpy to reload. They listened...nothing.

The wind was howling and seemed to be blowing Ben back a step for ever two he took. He stayed close to the bottom of the slope and was looking for the rope when he heard what sounded like a pistol and then again, he heard it. They were signaling him as to where they were. New strength surged through his body and him mind which had been shutting down came alive again.

"Help me God! Please give me strength," he prayed. He heard another shot, and it came from just above and behind him. He had passed the rope and did not see it. He struggled with numb fingers to pull his pistol from his belt and then had to will his thumb to pull the hammer back and pull the trigger.

The men heard the shot. "He's right below us," Jim said. As soon as the words were out of his mouth Buff was scrambling down the slope holding on to the rope. Reaching the bottom, he found Ben who was on all fours struggling to move. He grabbed Ben under the arm and lifted him up. He tied the rope around his friend's waist and jerked on the rope. Jim and stumpy begin pulling Ben up and Buff struggled up the now slippery slope behind Ben trying to keep him upright.

A few minutes later Jim had hold of Ben and he and Stumpy helped him around the bend and to the fire. Buff was right behind them. They stripped Ben's wet clothes off his shivering body and lay him next to the fire on a buffalo robe and a wool blanket over his shivering body. They wiped the ice off his face and beard and gave him some jerky that had been soaked in warm water and was easy to chew. Ben slowly chewed the almost tasteless meat slowly and swallowed. He opened his eyes for the first time.

"I thought I had died, and an angel was feeding me till I opened my eyes and saw your ugly face," Ben mumbled and forcing a smile. "No way God would let anyone be an angel with that face." Everyone laughed at that remark, even Ben struggled to smile.

"Well of all the ungrateful things to say to a man who just fed you," Jim said laughing and slapping Ben on the shoulder. "You just take it easy big boy. We don't want you to come down with a cough and lung congestion and fever. You just lie here by the fire for a couple days and get your strength back.

Ben nodded and fell immediately asleep.

Chapter Twenty-five

Ben slept off and on for the next forty-eight hours waking up only to eat and relieve his bladder. On the morning of the third day he awoke to voices that seemed to be in a mild disagreement. He listened.

"I thank we shud jus sta here fur a kuple mor days," Buff said.

Jim said. "I agree but the problem is we need meat, the horses are getting low on grass, and the firewood is getting low. We'd be in a hell of a fix if another storm hits unexpectedly and the clouds are looking heavy again." It was quite for a minute and then Jim spoke again. "I have enough sinew to make a bow string and I can find mountain juniper to make a bow from and I have a couple arrows wrapped in my blanket that I took that were stuck in the ground the last time we had a fight with the Blackfoot. Between you and me we could make a pretty good bow. I could find a deer or elk and not have to fire my Hawken."

"Tha may work, Jim. I don't like tha idee uf makin a lot uf noise whut whith with thos Red Sticks clos by."

Ben raised up. "What Redskins?"

"By jove he is alive," Jim chuckled then added. "We had a small of band of Blackfoot ride below the cave yesterday. It was a hunting party and they and not a war party. They were looking for game and not trappers otherwise one of them would have found something that told them white men were close and we would have been in for a fight."

"Anything to eat?" Ben asked?

Everyone laughed including Ben. Buff chuckled. "Heer we ar in a sitsation an this heer yungun is hungree." He reached over and slapped Ben on the shoulder. "Glad yu ar feelin better Ben. I'll git yu sum jerkee."

Ben looked and asked if it was morning or evening. "About midmorning Ben. Still cloudy but the wind and snow has stopped," Stumpy answered.

He threw the wool blanket off and being butt naked he reached over grabbed his pants that were hanging on a rock jutting out of the cave wall and slipped them on followed by his knee high moccasins and his wool shirt.

"Well," he said. "Let's get some grass and wood while you make a bow," looking at Jim.

"Who made yu booshway uf this soree outfit?" Buff asked smiling.

"What's a booshway?" Ben asked.

The other three trappers laughed at the question.

"Boss, leader, or whatever of a party of trappers," Jim replied.

Ben, embarrassed, said. "I... I didn't mean to make out I was. Jim, you just said we need to do those things while the weather was nice."

"That I did, Ben. That I did." He laughed and added. "We were just joshing you my friend: just having a little fun."

"Oh." Then I am going to get started and headed for the entrance.

"Yu furgetten aneethang thar, Sunnee?"Buff hollered after him. "Sumthang like yur kote in kase tha weaher sets in again or maybe yur pistols in kase yu run inta a bear or Injun."

Ben stooped and turned around rather embarrassed. "I forgot."

"Fergetting kan git a man kilt damn quik out here," Buff said tossing Ben's coat to him.

By late afternoon they had plenty of grass and wood. They squatted at the entrance of the cave, Buff puffing on his pipe and Ben and Stumpy watching for sign of Jim who had left four hours earlier with his bow strung across his back and all of his weapons.

"It's starting to snow again," Ben said looking up at the heavy grey clouds. "Hope Jim is close to here?"

Buff who had been sitting cross-legged against the cave wall stood up and looked out.

"Damn tha luk! he stated loudly.   "It's kumin' again." Ben and Stumpy looked where the old trapper was pointing. They could see the white wall of snow moving toward them. "This heree is gonnaa be wurse than befor."

They could hear the wind now even though it was probably more than a mile away. Ben went back into the cave and came out with his buffalo robe on and gloves.

"Whatcha thank yur gonna do?" Buff asked.

"I'm going to go down and hang on to the rope at the bottom and wait for Jim and make sure he don't miss it like did. He's going to need help getting up the slope especially if he has meat."

"Wal," Buff mumbled. "Problee a gud idee but don't yu let go uf that thar rope."

"I won't," Ben said and slid over the edge and scooted down the slope holding on to the rope.

A half mile away Jim was walking back along the creek carrying he hind quarters of a deer. He saw the wall of snow coming down the canyon and picked up the pace. *I don't have a prayer of getting to the cave before that hits*, he thought. He was still a few hundred yards away when the storm struck. In an instant he could not see more than five or six feet and the wind was like a knife cutting through him. He dropped the venison and pulled his robe tight around his chest and put his gloves on. Picking up the venison he continued his trek along the creek but holding close to the slope.

His lungs were burning like fire and his breathing was fast and he felt like he was not getting enough air when he sucked in the precious stuff. His legs were giving out on him and his head was spinning. He sat down with his back to the wind which helped. He fumbled to get his pistol out and managed to fire a shot in the air.

Ben damned near jumped out of his buffalo robe. The shot was fired almost next to him. He pulled his pistol and fired it in the air. Jim stood up and turned back into the wind took two more steps and saw a shape before him no more than four steps away.

Ben saw him at the same time and holding on to the rope took a step and reached out and grabbed Jim's extended hand. He took Jim's gloved hand and tied the rope around his arm.

He leaned over and cupped his hands and yelled in Jim's ear. "Hold on. Let me have the meat." He gave some hard jerks on the rope and was relieved when it got tight and Jim was being pulled up the slope. He struggled behind. It took twenty minutes to get himself and Jim to the cave opening even with Buff and Stumpy pulling hard. They managed to get to the fire and all four collapsed in exhaustion.

Ben rolled over and wiped the snow and ice from Jim's beard and eyebrows. He stripped the wet clothes from Jim's shivering body and like they did him laid him on a robe and placed a wool blanket over him pulling it up under his chin. Picking up a cup he went over to Buff's possibles bag and took out the flask of whiskey. He was shivering also, and the cup was shaking in his hand as he poured in a little of the rotgut.

He moved back over to Jim and kneeling down lifted his head a little and placed the cup between his lips. He poured a little down Jims' throat and immediately Jim's eyes flew open and he started coughing and wheezing.

Buff and Stumpy had raised up to see what was going on and heard Jim cussing Ben. He suddenly stopped, smiled, and taking the cup the cup drank the rest in a couple gulps feeling the warmth spread from his belly to the rest of his body.

"Well, I killed my first deer with a bow."

"Yep, and durned neer froze ta death doing it. If'n it hadn't been fur Ben yu wud have been as stiff as a bord by now. Them thar old grey eyeballs uf yourn jus starrin up at tha sky not seein nuthen."

They all laughed, and Jim put his hand on Ben's shoulder. "Thanks Ben," he said. "Thanks."

"Whut abut ole Stump and me? We danged neer pulled out sholders out us soketts pulling yur soree ass up that thar slope."

"Thanks to all of you. I was almost down for the count. Think that was about the closest I ever came to freezing to death. Been cold before but not to the point I didn't think I was going to make it. Thanks again."

Chapter Twenty-six

The days and weeks went by with today the same as yesterday and will be the same tomorrow: pull grass for the horses, find firewood and try to find meat to eat.

On this morning Jim said. "This cave has been a Godsend to us ole' boys but I figure its late February or maybe early March and we are having to go too far to find firewood, grass and game." He looked at Buff. "What do you think? Do we need to move on upstream and find another place to hold up till spring thaw?"

Buff took another sip of coffee in the damnable tin cup before speaking.

"I've been thanking abut that fur a few days, Jim and I agree. We're walkin nigh on a mile now jus ta find wud and grass. I kno yu ar going a lot further ta find meet." He took another sip of coffee. "I'm fer movin on and find us a nu plac ta hole up."

Jim looked at Stumpy and Ben who both nodded their agreement. By late morning they had made it down the slippery slope without incident mainly to Ben's strong back along with Stumpy holding taught a rope around the pommel of the saddle on their mounts and tied to the wooden cross pieces of the racks on the pack animals to help keep from sliding and falling. It had taken over three hours to get the animals down one at a time.

Weeks and months passed without incident except one for spell when it snowed for a week, but they had found another cave to hole up in. It was not near as large as the first one, but it worked out nicely.

It was spring now and the deep snow was melting away and the streams were running with fresh cold water. They had trapped some when the weather permitted but now was the best time while the beaver still had their heavy coats of fur on and these would bring top dollar at the rendezvous. There was always a chance of a storm blowing this early in spring, but it was a chance trapper had to take.

Of course, unexpected storms were not the only danger trappers had to watch for because spring brought the terror of the mountains...the grizzly out from hibernation and he would be hungry and in a nasty mood. Add bands of Utes and Blackfoot hunting parties moving about and it was simply a dangerous time.

The four had a base camp located deep in a deadfall of huge pines which they were almost invisible to anyone traveling close to it. With all the dead trees they didn't have to look for firewood and the stream which was over fifty yards wide at this point was at their back. It was only two to three-foot-deep but would definitely slow an attacking party of unfriendly strangers be they red or white. Using ropes tied to a couple of the dead pines they had pulled them between their camp and the stream with their pack horse. This would offer added protection if an attack came from that direction. Looking at it the two most experienced trappers were satisfied. They had defensible camp and a whole lot of beaver in the stream.

After two weeks each one of the men had an average of forty-five plews each which was damn good money considering the quality of the pelts.

True to his belief in not taking all the beaver in an area Jim had decided to move on farther up the stream. Squatted by the small fire this night he made his decision to the others.

"Yall know how I feel, and Buff too, about trapping out an area. I think we need to pull in our traps in the morning and move on. If anyone disagrees, we can discuss it. Anyone?" No one said anything but all three nodded their heads in approval. "It's a done thing then. We'll get out traps at first light after taking care of any beaver we have and then move on." With that said they moved to their bedrolls. Their horses were very close with each hobbled and with their hearing and sense of smell would be excellent night guards.

The next morning, they ran their traps and picked up their traps. Only Stumpy and Buff had beaver, so it was a sign it was time to move on.

They were in process of breaking camp when they heard rifle shots, running horses and yipping of Indians. Jim stepped out of the deadfall to get a look-see as to what was going on. He saw five trappers laying low in the saddle with pack horses being chased by about thirty or so what looked like Utes.

He fired his long gun and waved his hat. The trappers seeing him turned their horses toward the deadfall where Jim stood waving his hat. Reaching where Jim was, they reined in their horses so hard they sat on their haunches sliding to a stop in a cloud of dust.

Buff, Ben and Stumpy had their Hawkins and fired into the Utes emptying three ponies of their riders. The rest surprised at the other trappers swerved away to take council on what to do with this new situation.

The trappers had dismounted even before their mounts came to a complete stop jumping from them with their long guns in one hand and the reins in the other and were pulling their horses into the safety of the thick deadfall.

One of the trappers who was as tall as Ben but not near as thick threw the shoulders shouted when he saw Buff and Jim.

"Damnation boys, it's good to see you." He walked over to Buff. "How you doing Buff you old buffalo turd!" He shook Buff's hand and looked over at his friend Jim Bridger. He shook Jim's hand. "Never been so glad to see someone in my life, Jim."

"Good to see you Will. Where did you pick up your friends," he said nodding to where the Utes were bunched up about three hundred yards away?"

"About two miles back," he replied while he, Jim and the others were reloading. He was interrupted by a shout from Buff.

"Here they come!"

All conversation stopped as everyone rushed to get behind the downed trunks of the pines. The noise of pounding horse's hooves and the war cries of the Utes would have made it impossible to hear one another anyway. The Utes were charging across a meadow that was maybe a quarter mile across with knee high grass.

Nine men, all excellent shots fired almost as one when the Utes were seventy-five or so yards out and there were few misses. The deadly volley did not deter the remaining Utes as they were almost on the trappers when each man used their short guns and again several warriors were knocked off their war ponies. This second volley turned the charge and they returned to where they were before the charge: just out of range of the trapper's long guns.

"LOOK AT THAT," one of the trappers that came in with named Will yelled.

All looked where he was pointing.

"Damnation," Will cursed.

As they watched maybe thirty or more Utes showed up. They were now looking at fifty or sixty warriors and would have been a lot more if they hadn't knocked down fifteen or so earlier and no one knew if those were dead or lying in the grass wounded and crawling toward them thru the high grass.

Jim hollered at Stumpy who was on the opposite end of the deadfall. "Make sure all of the horses are deep in the deadfall and away from any stray arrows or bullets." So far, he had seen no Ute with anything but bows but that didn't mean the bunch that just come in didn't have any guns they had taken from trappers they had killed.

He turned to Will. "We are in a pickle here Will. With that bunch that just come in we are outnumbered about five or so to one. I think we may be able to hold them off if they charge again but I think they know we are not going anywhere and may not risk a direct attack and lose a lot of braves."

"We are in a good defensive position," Will replied, "And water will be no problem with the creek right behind us, but food may be if they keep us pinned down here for a while."

"Do you have any food with you?"

"Have some jerky and plenty of coffee and a few biscuits."

Jim looked across the meadow. "Looks like they are going to be here for a while. They are making some campfires and putting their horses out to graze."

"I don't know if that's good news or bad news." Will chuckled. "Sorry we got you in this mess Jim."

"Don't fret none over that. You would have done the same for me or any trappers that were in the situation ya'll were in. None of us want to see any trapper killed or caught and tortured by any of the tribes especially the Utes."

"Amen to that," one of the men that came in with Will said. "I saw a man that had been captured or at least what looked like a man. There wasn't much left when they got through with him."

"Glad you and Buff are here," one of the other men said. "Heard a lot of stories about you two."

"Don't go ta beleevin evree storee yu heer," Buff said.

Jim cleared his throat. "To get back to the problem we have. We need to go through our possible bags and packs to see what food each of us have. I think it would be a good idea for Buff to hold it and dish it out sparingly so it will last as long as possible."

"Good idea, Jim." Get to it men and give what you have to Buff there," Will said.

A few minutes Buff was taking stock: two pounds of coffee, pound of sugar, some flour, salt and pepper, and about two pounds of jerky.

"If'in we are heer for mor'n two daz we will be out uf food," Buff mumbled just loud enough for the men to hear him. "Aint gud."

"We'll make do," the always positive Jim said. "Right now, we need to check our weapons and then rest up. We need to have two watching at all times. Will, you set the schedule for two hours a shift. Will, you and me will take the last one just before daylight.

Ben rekindled the fire they had put out earlier when they were preparing to break camp. He put the coffee on. He squatted there and thinking, *sixty of them or so to nine of us-I wonder if any of us will see the next sunrise.*

Chapter Twenty-seven

The night passed quietly-if you could call listening to continuous screaming of the dancing warriors around a huge fire quiet. At least there were no attacks on us.

Dawn came with nine trappers tired and sleepy. Jim had all of us up and behind the trunk of the big pine.

"If they are going to come it will be when the sun breaks over the tops of the mountains in front of us so it will be in our eyes."

Ben was wide awake and as always ready for a fight. He kneeled behind the log with Buff on his right and Stumpy second man on his left. The Utes were mounting their war ponies and preparing for an all-out attack that would overwhelm them for sure. One, apparently the war chief was prancing his pony back and forth screaming at his braves and waving his rifle above his head getting them more excited.

"I don't thank them Red Sticks need ta git anee more wurked up," Buff said loud enough for Ben to hear.

Jim shouted suddenly. "When they charge everyone shoot at the one doing the prancing back and forth. He's their war chief and if he goes down, they might just withdraw long enough to elect another."

The war chief turned his pony toward the trappers and waving his rifle, the only one the tappers could see they had, let out a war cry and the attack began. Sixty or so horses make a lot of noise even on the grass of the meadow they were charging across not to mention the war hoops and screams of the warriors. It was enough to make the ordinary man want to crawl off and hide.

The trappers however were not ordinary men, and they held their rifles steady, all aimed at the one Jim pointed out. At just under one hundred yards the men opened up. They could see the leader blown backwards and somersaulted to the ground hitting hard and rolling a couple times and then just lay there. Two braves directly behind their leader were swept off their mounts by bullets intended for their leader.

The charge halted temporarily giving the trappers a few seconds to reload their rifles and get set for the final charge. The Utes started back to their camp to the surprise, and excitement, of the men behind the logs.

They were patting Jim on the back and on the shoulders. Finally, Will Spoke.

"How did you know that Jim? I've been out here as long as you and been in fights before but did not know that.

"Jeb Smith mentioned that to me at the rendezvous last year. He was in a fight with the Utes and someone shot the one that was stirring them up and leading the attack when they turned and rode away. He figured the other warriors thought their leader did not have the right "medicine" or that his medicine was bad."

"Who knows what goes on in the head of an Injun?" One of the men with Will said then added. "We all know how notional they are. Hell, one minute they may let you in their camp like you were an old friend then slit your throat during the night. Never will trust one of them as long as I live."

Ben spoke up. "That may not be long friend," he said nodding across the meadow at the gathering warriors.

The sun was well over the mountain tops now. There was not a cloud in the sky and the only thing moving besides the Utes were a few buzzards circling overhead.

Ben looked up at the buzzards and mumbled. "Looks like they are expecting lunch later today."

"Let's hope its them thar Utes tha ar feestin on and not trapp'r meet," Buff chuckled.

Ben turned his head and looked at his friend and wondered how in blazes anyone could make a joke at a time like this then realized staying calm is probably why he and Jim have survived out here for so long.

They were charging fast and laying low on the backs of their ponies giving the trappers as small a target as possible. Seeing this Jim shouted for the men to shoot the ponies. Seven or eight went down with the first volley throwing their riders violently to the ground. One of the riders thrown was the one leading the charge, but they did not slow this time.

The trappers fired their pistols and then their second pistol taking a fearsome toll on the Utes. They turned twenty yards out and unleashed their arrows as they swooped across the ground in front of the trappers.

The man on his right, the one who said no Indian could not be trusted, took an arrow in the forehead and was killed instantly. Ben had an arrow slice painfully thru the top of his left shoulder. He heard a grunt from down the line and knew another trapper had been hit. He did not have time to worry about who it was as ten or twelve of the Utes jumped from the backs of their racing ponies and rolling on the ground came up running and throwing themselves at the trappers with tomahawks and knives slashing.

Ben planted his hatchet in the forehead of one diving over the trunk of the dead pine splitting the man's head open. The weight of the warrior's lifeless body crashing to the ground jerked the hatchet which was stuck in the man's head from his grip.

Ben didn't have time as another Ute was almost on top him and was already in the process of swinging his tomahawk at his head. Ben dropped into a crouch and ducked his head just as the blade took his hat off. The Ute's forward momentum was taking him over and past the trapper, but Ben had drawn his butcher knife slashed upward and the razor-sharp blade cut deep into the man's thigh.

Ben raised himself and turned to face the wounded man only to see the side of the injured warrior's head being caved in by the swinging weight of a Hawken rifle by Buff. The two trappers nodded at each other for an instant and then was back into the life or death struggle they were in.

In that brief instant Ben saw Jim drive his butcher knife into the chest of another Ute. The remaining warriors had had enough and were leaping over the trunk to get away. Ben who had practiced long and hard with throwing his butcher knife let it fly at the closest Ute and saw it go deep between the shoulder blades of the man. One of the other trappers had managed to reload his pistol or maybe had not fired it in the first place blasted another in the back killing him.

The area in front of the deadfall where the trappers as well as behind it was a sight no one wanted to see. Dead warriors littered the area in front and dead ones behind it. The man to Ben's left was dead with the arrow in the forehead, eyes open with an astonished look on his face as he had died instantly. One farther down had an arrow in his chest and probably would be gone pretty quick as a lot of frothy blood was spilling from his lips indicating the arrow had penetrated a lung.

Buff and Jim both came out the fight with no injuries. Ben had the scrape on his shoulder and Stumpy had a bloody head from a glancing blow of a tomahawk. Will had a knife wound in his left shoulder and two of the other had wounds but none disabling. They all reloaded their rifles and pistols, and Ben loaded the weapons of the man who had died beside him. He saw Stumpy, his head wrapped in a piece of shirt he had ripped apart, loading the man's weapons who had the arrow in his chest.

Ben ran outside the deadfall and retrieved his knife from the dead warriors back wiping the blade on the man's breechcloth and hurried back to the deadfall. The men gathered around Jim and a sorry looking lot they were but looks can be deceiving. Besides Jim and Buff, every man was bleeding from somewhere on their body but they were not down and out: a long way from it as they were fighting men and they would do what they needed to do to survive. This was not the first time each one had faced death and survived.

Jim said. "Don't think this is over men because it ain't. We killed too many of them for them just to ride off. They want to finish the job they started just for revenge sake. I figure we have cut their numbers by almost half, but we are down to seven. Due to the number we have killed I don't think they will try another frontal, but they will figure out something I just don't know what. Any of you have any ideas?"

No one said anything till Ben spoke up. "Reckon they know we are low on food? If they do I figure they will just stall and try to starve us out."

"Mabee," Buff said. "Tha got theer mad up an sumtimes when Injuns git their mad up tha don't have tha normal patshens tha usualy do ta wate."

"You both are right," Jim said. "So, I guess the best thing, the only thing that is, we can do is try to make ourselves comfortable as we can after we take care of the dead and wounded. We also need to get the dead Utes out from behind the deadfall and put them with the ones in front so they can be picked up. They have great respect for their dead so they will come to get them. As a matter of fact, this is what we will do to show them we also have respect for a fighting man."

He told the men." We will gather up the dead and place them gently, with respect, in a line with their arms folded across their chest." Then he added. "Make damn sure they are dead before you pick them up if you don't want a knife stuck in your ribs." They went to work to clean things up.

Chapter Twenty-eight

The rest of the day passed quietly. A small group of Utes after a sign language meeting with Jim picked up the dead bodies of their brothers without incident. Just before the sun disappeared behind the mountains Ben built up the fire and they sit around sipping hot coffee and chewing what jerky Buff has rationed out.

"What do you think Jim? Those Utes done are they still going to try to finish us off?" Will asked.

"No," Jim emphatically answered. "This is not over by a long shot. Tonight, we need two men on guard duty with two-hour shifts. Will, you set the schedule. Ben, you go make sure the horses are secure. I don't think they will try anything tonight but will wait for first light again. They don't like to fight at night but don't count on that being set in stone. Utes are like all the other tribes up here in the mountains, unpredictable."

Ben left the cozy warmth of the fire and walked back to where the horses were deep in the deadfall. The logs were stacked six to eight feet high forming a perfect holding place. His horse came over to him and nuzzled his shoulder while Ben scratched him between the ears. He was satisfied with the horse situation and after a minute of scratching his horse walked back to the others.

"Things appear good back there," he said out loud to no one in particular.

It was full dark, and the coffee was just about gone so Ben made another pot, so he and the others had coffee when they were on duty. Two of Will's men had the first watch so everyone else finished what was in the cups and were off to their bedrolls.

Ben was dead tired, and his left shoulder pained him some and he found sleep hard to come by. He lay on the ground cloth that had his wool blanket on it with his head on his saddle. He had his buffalo robe on top of him as the night chill was already setting in. It was early September, and the days were still warming up right nice but once the sun disappeared the nights began to get quite cold. Even this time of the year it would sometimes drop below freezing.

Someone was already snoring as he lay there looking up at the night sky. It was a cloudless night, and the stars were starting to appear. He found some of the constellations his dad had pointed out to him when he was growing up when they would sometimes camp out. He missed his folks a considerable amount but he had made the decision to come out here and God only knows he does not regret his decision. He knew now what a dangerous place it was where death could come at any time but that only made it more intriguing. He loved the mountains, the pines, the beautiful aspens, the clear clean air, and he loved the freedom of being his own boss. Nope, he would not change a thing and then he chuckled to himself, *except maybe the way Buff talked that made it hard for most to figure what the hell he was saying most of the time.* With that thought he finally drifted off to a restless sleep.

About midnight he awakens with a hand shaking his shoulder.

"Your time Ben," one of the newcomers said. "Things are quite...almost too quiet."

Ben stood up, picked up his Hawken and walked to the coals of what was left of the small fire and filled his tin cup with coffee. Will, having been woke up, walked up and filled his cup.

"I'll watch the horses for a while and then we will switch if that's okay with you?" He said. Ben nodded and took the three steps to the logs that faced the meadow. Across the meadow he could see the small fires of the Utes. He counted four. Earlier while lying on his bedroll he could hear the chanting or yelling or whatever the Utes were doing, but it was all quite now. In fact, it was too quite just like the man who woke him up said. There was not even a breeze to ruffle the leaves of the aspens that lined the creek. He moved quietly to where Will was watching the horses. In almost a whisper he said.

"I have a feeling the Utes are up to no good. I think they are getting as close as they can under the cover of darkness and hit us at dawn and they will be so close that we will get one shot each, maybe not even that, before they over run us."

"What do you figure on doing?"

"Scout the area in front and see if I can find out."

"Damn Ben. That's the dumbest thing I ever heard. That's suicide."

"Do you want to wake up with a knife in your gut? I know it's risky, but we can't afford to be surprised in the morning I hate to wake up everyone and then it be a false alarm. I'm pretty good at sneaking around so I'll be fine. Just stay here with your Hawken in case I do stir up trouble and you can cover me."

Will nodded. "I still think it's the craziest thing I ever heard."

With that said, Ben slipped over the huge log, got on his belly with his butcher knife in his right hand and began to move away from the deadfall. His heart was pounding and even though it was chilly he found himself sweating. The grass was two-foot-high and raising himself up from the ground enough that he could see over the top of the grass he looked. His eyes were accustomed to the darkness, but he still could not see more than two or three feet on this moonless night.

He would move ever so slow and quite only a couple feet at a time then stop, listen and look around. It was at one of these stops he heard a sound. He could not figure out what it was at first. Straining his ears, he heard it again ever so faintly. What was it? He held his breath not moving anything but his eyes and gripping the knife tight. The sound came again, and he knew what it was: leather scraping the ground. He was right and silently started to move slowly back to the camp.

With what seemed like an eternity he was at the log and raised himself up after quietly calling Will's name so he would not shoot him when he came over the log. When he swung his body over, he was surprised to see Jim and Buff there with Will.

"They are out there. I dammed near met one face to face crawling toward us."

"He didn't see or hear you?" Jim whispered.

"No."

"That thar wus the craziest thang I ever hurd uf yu damn fool but abut tha bravest thang to. Problee saved us too." Buff whispered putting his hand on Ben's shoulder.

Ben was shocked he had been gone as long as he had. Ben and Buff had woken up to take their turn watching and Will had told them what he had done. It was an hour before dawn, so all the men were up. They had their long guns loaded and each had a brace of pistols loaded and cocked and their knives stuck in the pine log within easy and quick reach. They waited.

Chapter Twenty-nine

They came with a rush just as the sky was turning grey. They were shocked when a barrage of lead balls tore into their ranks followed immediately with another volley with devastating effect. So shocked were the Utes they fell back toward their camp. They had apparently been so sure of their surprise they only had their knives and tomahawks with them expecting only close in fighting. They left nine of their brothers dead or seriously wounded behind.

The trappers were quickly reloading their weapons as only a tenderfoot would go about after firing his weapon and not reloading immediately. They watched intently as the Utes were in a circle listening to their war chief who was shouting at them loud enough for the white men to hear.

"Wish I knew the Ute lingo," Ben mumbled.

"Yeah," Will said. "I'd give a pack of plews to know what was being said."

"It's purty simple," Buff said. "He's jus say'n we gonna kill them thar white sumbitches if'n it's tha last thang we do."

Even though things were tense the men had to smile at the old trapper for his sense of humor, but they pretty much knew that was probably what was being said. As they watched a single Ute approached them holding his lance above his head. He approached to about forty feet from the deadfall and then stabbed his lance into the ground. It had red feathers on the butt end and the slight wind stirred them and they fluttered with it. The Ute shouted at them. Probably some Ute obscenities and rode back to the others.

One of Will's men asked. "What was that all about?"

"Damnation! Look at that," Will shouted as they saw a group of fifteen or so join the others.

"I think I know what they are going to do," Jim said. Make yourselves as small as possible and hug the log. As he said it about twenty-five or thirty arrows filled the air arching high in the air toward them. As they watched death rain down, they were relieved the arrows fell just short.

They watched as the line of warriors moved their ponies forward a few paces.

"Aim over their heads some and let loose boys then grab dirt." They fired their long guns just as another volley of arrows headed their way. Jim saw two Ute fall slump and fall over their ponies and one pony went down throwing its rider.

This time the arrows were barely short with some sticking into to log they were behind.

"Sumbitches," one of the men down the line of trappers yelled out. Why don't they just charge and try to overrun us."

"Tha dun tried that. Didn't work out to well fer them." They quickly reloaded again.

"This round will be dead on men so make yourselves small as soon as you fire them rifles." They watched the Utes move up a few more paces.

"Fire," Jim hollered as the warriors were stretching their strings on their bows fixing to let loose the deadly missiles. The men fired almost as one just as the arrows were loosed. Four more warriors were sent to the happy hunting ground or whatever they believed they went when dead.

The arrows arched high and came almost straight down. Ben heard the shafts hitting the log and the ground and he head the unmistakable sound of some hitting flesh followed by curses and grunts of the men hit. Two of Wills men were dead each having two arrows in their backs and one of them had one in his leg also.

"Reload!" Jim shouted, "And fire again." He knew if they didn't the Utes were charge again and over run them for sure.

Ben, Stumpy, Jim, Will, and Buff all fired again saw three more knocked from their ponies.

Once again arrows arched into the sky and rained down on the remaining trappers and falling among them. Will had one stuck plumb through his calf and one in the back of his shoulder. Stumpy had one in his thigh and Ben had deep gash in his upper right arm where one had sliced thru it before sticking into the ground. Buff and Jim remained unscathed.

Reloading again they fired their long rifles and pistols knocking four more off their ponies and had a couple hanging on their pony's manes to keep from falling off.

Things didn't look to good for the trappers. Ben was thinking about home. *Probably never see ma and pa again nor his brother and sisters. Probably should have never left them*, then he erased that thought. *If I die today it would be okay. I will die doing what I have wanted to do, and I would change nothing.* He looked across the stream and up at the high peaks still heavy with snow. *That's the most beautiful sight I ever did see.* He tried to remember a prayer from his youth that his momma used to say all the time when trouble came. *Yea though I walk through the valley of death* and something about still waters and *then I will fear no evil because thou art with me. He wished he could remember all of it. He wished he could remember his ma's face.*

"Here they come again, "Jim shouted. The men looked up and saw the deadly shafts raining down on them. "Make yourself small," Jim shouted which was easy for him and Buff who neither weighed more than one fifty or so pounds. Not so for Ben and Will who were both over six foot and one eighty to two hundred or so pounds each.

The arrows hit and Ben cursed as one stuck in his calf. He heard Will grunt and either Buff or Jim also to his right. He had his pistols reloaded and he raised himself up and fired twice and saw one of the warriors pitch backwards off his pony. Jim fired once and then ducked back down. Will was dead, two arrows in his back and one in his hip. Jim had one high in his hip. So far Buff had not been scratched.

Buff looked over the log. "They are fixing to fire another round."

Jim scrambled the best he could to where Ben was. " Pull the dead over yourselves and reload your pistols," which was quicker than the long guns. "Stumpy, you roll far as you can to your left. Jim, Buff, and Ben pulled the dead men on top of them and started reloading. The arrows begin hitting all around them and they could feel the arrows hitting their dead friends' bodies. They also hear something else. Gunfire and lots of it.

They threw the bodies off their selves and looked over the log to the prettiest sight any of them had ever seen. The Utes were running away as a group of about fifteen or so trappers came charging into view yelling and firing their weapons.

Buff stood up yelling and waving his hat. The trappers turned and slowed their horses to a walk and headed toward them.

Jim, Ben, and Stumpy stood as best they could and waved also.

A minute later the men halted their horses in front of the deadfall.

"I be damned," the man in front of the others said. "Jim Bridger and Buff."

"Howdy Les," Jim said then added. "Don't believe I have ever been so glad to see someone in my life.

Les looked around at the dead Utes lying on the ground and at other blood spots that had dried up. He dismounted and walked to where Jim and Buff were and extended his hand which Buff shook vigorously.

"This here ole boy says tha same thang Les. Dang glad ta see ya," Buff said smiling all the time.

"Looks like you boys had your hand full here." Then he saw the bodies with all the arrows in them. "More than a handful I'd say."

"We were goners," Jim said. "You showing up when you did saved our sorry hides."

"I guess you boys owe me one then," Les chuckled. "Really Jim, I'm just glad we come along. We heard all the shooting and figured there were trappers in trouble."

Buff said. "We wur shor nuff in truble I'll give yu that."

"Ya'll headed to the rendezvous?" Jim asked.

"Yep." He saw the arrow in Jim's hip and in Ben and Stumpy. "Why don't we get you doctored up and ya'll just tag along with us. Be a lot safer. Only a dumbass redskin would attack twenty or so trappers and I don't think I have ever met an Indian that was dumb," he chuckled.

Three hours later they were on their way. The arrows had been removed and all was good except for Jim. The arrow came out but the tip stayed high in his hip. One of the trappers with Les, a Frenchman, was pretty good but try as he might the tip was just too deep.

Note: The tip would stay in his hip till the rendezvous of 1836 when a real medical doctor came through with a wagon train. The doctor found it was a metal tip not flint and had adhered to the hip bone. It had to be broken off

with forceps which having no other pain killer than whiskey was quite an ordeal for the mountain man to endure but only was a testimony to the strength and courage the trappers had.

The wounds to Ben and Stumpy were painful but a little whiskey had helped ease the discomfort some. Jim was a different situation: riding a horse with an arrow tip in your hip was more than uncomfortable, it was plain out painful every step the horse took, and whiskey hadn't helped a whole lot. They had folded a blanket to put on the saddle that was helpful but not much. The men offered to make a travois for him to lay on but Jim, the prideful man he was refused.

It would have been better if they could have waited a couple days for the wounds to get a little better but no one wanted to stay there and risk a very large party of Utes showing up to avenger their dead brothers. No one really believed they would but why take the chance.

The first night the wounds were cleaned with more rot gut much to the hollering and cussing of the men it was used on.

"Damn Jim," Les said. "I've known you for a long time and didn't know you knew those words." Everyone laughed and even Jim had to smile...just a little one though.

The horses had been taken care of, the coffee made and the men squatted around the two fires...all but

Jim, Ben, and Stumpy as they lay on their blankets sipping coffee laced with a little rot gut to give it the proper flavor.

The Frenchman, Alexandre Boucher, thought the wounds looked good and so far, showed no signs of infection.

The talk was mostly about the rendezvous they were headed to and occasionally the dang Utes and Blackfoot. The group that was led by Les were company men, meaning they worked for the fur companies and Jim's group were free trapper meaning they worked for themselves. There was no love lost between the groups and often there were serious conflicts between them, but Jim and Les were old friends and things were okay...so far.

The days passed and finally they were at the rendezvous. Several trappers were already there and lots from various tribes of friendly Indians, namely Nez Pearce, Crow, Flatheads, and Shoshone.

The furs of the men killed at the battle at the deadfall were divided equally among Jim, Buff, Ben and Stumpy. They did not give Les and his men any because they would just have given them to the fur company they worked for, the Rocky Mountain Fur Company, that would be at the rendezvous.

Ben's first year was a profitable one with him having almost three hundred pelts of his own and another one hundred from his dead friends. He made about fourteen hundred dollars and had over four hundred left after buying what he would need for the next year from the merchants that were there.

Being recently from the states he was shocked at how high the prices were, even higher than the year before. He understood somewhat after Jim explained why. The merchants had to travel a month over land from St. Louis and then a month back which resulted in a lot of expenses in travel with having to pay drivers and men to help guard the valuable merchandise in their wagons.

Ben thought his first full year had been a great learning experience and looked forward to the coming year trapping with his new friends, Jim, Buff, and Stumpy. He knew they were going to have some great and maybe not so great times: Some fun times and probably some dangerous times. He smiled at the thought. He was ready for his second year...but that's another story.

Gary McMillan

Book 13 of the

Tye Watkins Series

Thanks to the help of Tye in the past and Lt. Bullis and his black Seminole Scouts of late the Apache problem along the Texas/Mexico Border has slowed to an occasional small band of young bucks raising hell by the year of 1874.

However, the Comanche, mainly the Quahadi's, who were led by the most white hating of all Comanches, Quanah Parker. During the years of 1872 through 1874 millions of buffalo were killed by hide hunters almost wiping out the Plains Indians main source of food, clothing, tools, and hides for the teepees. Most of the various tribe surrendered to the army and placed on reservations including the Comanche-with the exception of the Quahadis.

The moved south and found the great canyon southwest of present day of Amarillo now called the Palo

Duro Canyon. This was perfect for them. The depth in places of 1000 feet and over a hundred miles long with water and game was made for them and they flourish and raided, and all was good.

Then a soldier, Captain Ranald Mackenzie or "bad hand" as the Indians called him due fingers being shot off, entered the picture ordered by Washington to bring an end to the Indian problem once and for all with whatever means he deemed necessary. Before he got a complete picture of what was happening is where my book begins. The Quahadis led by Quanah begin raiding south as far down as Fort Clark.

Tye, tired of being away from his family had turned in his marshal badge and was again a scout at Fort Clark much to the appreciation of Major Thurston and the troops at Clark. News of Comanche raiding parties had just reached the fort and patrols were being readied to find them.

This book will be available in three or four months.

Gary McMillan

www.ingramcontent.com/pod-product-compliance
Lightning Source LLC
Chambersburg PA
CBHW030533270626
47155CB00024B/3029